"You're leaving me."

"Only for as long as it takes to end this thing." He figured he had seconds only before he had to be ready for whatever came through that door. "I want you to know one thing."

He didn't touch her, because his control would break and right now he needed his mind in the game. But later everything would be different. "When this is over I'm going to kiss you. One of those long, sexy kisses that knock your shoes off and have you wondering why you ever bothered to kiss a man before me."

"You're awfully sure of yourself," Risa said.

"It comes from the slow buildup of simple dates to a complex disaster. This has been brewing. It's all wrapped up with adrenaline and excitement." He leaned in. "And now it's out of our control."

HELENKAY DIMON

SWITCHED

HARLEQUIN®
entertain, enrich, inspire™

To all the readers who have bought my Harlequin Intrigue
books and sent me such lovely notes and emails. Thank you!

ISBN-13: 978-0-373-69654-3

SWITCHED

Copyright © 2012 by HelenKay Dimon

Recycling programs
for this product may
not exist in your area.

ABOUT THE AUTHOR

Award-winning author HelenKay Dimon spent twelve years in the most unromantic career ever—divorce lawyer. After dedicating all that effort to helping people terminate relationships, she is thrilled to deal in happy endings and write romance novels for a living. Now her days are filled with gardening, writing, reading and spending time with her family in and around San Diego. HelenKay loves hearing from readers, so stop by her website, www.helenkaydimon.com, and say hello.

Books by HelenKay Dimon

CAST OF CHARACTERS

Aaron McBain—His outside security firm provides extra protection for a businessman someone wants dead. Aaron thinks the office Christmas party is a relatively low-risk atmosphere, but he's ready for anything. Then the bullets start flying and a woman he cares about but needs to forget wades right into the danger.

Risa Peters—Happy in her new job, Risa sets out to check a potential holiday party location and ends up in the wrong place at the wrong time. Mistaken for a woman she doesn't know, Risa is attacked and nearly kidnapped, only to be saved by the guy she once dated. And then things get scary....

Lowell Craft—The controversial businessman and owner of Craft Industries. Threats against his life turn a routine office Christmas party into a dangerous cat-and-mouse game, but is he as unconcerned as he appears?

Brandon Lowell—It's not easy being the son of a famous and wealthy man when your father treats you like an embarrassment.

Angie Troutman—She works at Craft Industries but is better known for the private time she spends with the boss after hours. She is at the center of the attack, the woman the kidnappers really want instead of Risa, but is everything what it seems?

Palmer Trask—The official security face of the company—his job is to keep Lowell safe. Palmer doesn't trust Aaron or anyone else. When the shooting starts, his decisions have an impact on everything that happens thereafter.

Royal Jenkins—Aaron's assistant and friend. He steps up when the danger begins, but could the threat be closer than any of them expect?

Chapter One

Aaron McBain stood in the only doorway without mistletoe taped to the beam and checked his watch for the tenth time. The schedule ticked along with precision. No surprises. No problems.

He knew that was a bad sign.

No holiday party ever ran on time or as planned. Actually, no party, meeting or anything sponsored by Craft Industries sailed along without an issue. But a half hour before the official kickoff, a steady line of sullen office workers dressed in gray suits filed in and now hovered in groups around tables and near the Christmas tree set up on the small stage at the far end of the room.

Absent was the usual happy holiday chatter found at similar events for other companies, likely because the boss declared attendance mandatory for this after-hours, nowhere-near-the-office party. Amazing how requiring people to have fun guaranteed they didn't.

Neither did the thirty-mile drive from their northern Virginia office building in McLean to the Elan Conference Center at the edge of the metro area's wine country in Loudoun County. Lowell Craft, the company's president and owner, lived out there and didn't care what kind of traffic disaster the Washington, D.C., rush hour imposed on everyone else.

Aaron wasn't exactly on fire for the party, either, and the drive was only one frustration. For the past three months, since he and his team had been hired by Lowell to provide him with extra security, he'd been handling everything from drunken rages in the office hallways by dismissed employees to outright threats against Lowell. And since Lowell spouted some controversial business theories, including one about how what motivated the staff was a series of unexpected firings on Fridays, it was amazing the guy wasn't attacked in the office parking lot every afternoon.

But there was a viable threat today, had been for months since Lowell got the first note promising a painful death if he didn't step down as head of the company by Christmas. Which was why Aaron stood three feet away from where Lowell inspected the buffet table, wearing his usual frown. He apparently didn't approve of the festive atmosphere the center had provided. Not a surprise to Aaron since as far as he could tell Lowell didn't like anything.

Aaron blew out a long breath as he listened to his assistant, Royal Jenkins, whistle an annoying tune into the open-ear mic. When the frustrated exhale didn't drive the point home, Aaron tried an across-the-room scowl at the man who was younger, fitter and less disciplined but possessed sniper-level shooting skills thanks to his short army stint.

Finally Aaron went for the direct approach with Royal. "Any chance you could stop that?"

"You want to request a different song?" Royal smiled as he nodded a welcome to Angie Troutman, the woman who by day ran the Craft human resources department and by night serviced Lowell. Their evening activities were a constant source of office gossip.

"Let's start with a moment of silence and then go from there," Aaron said.

Royal walked across the room and two seconds later stood next to Aaron. "You notice something missing at this party?"

Aaron watched the employees crowd together at a point in the room farthest away from their boss. "People who actually want to be here?"

"There is that, but no."

"Is it the lack of anything resembling holiday cheer or happiness?"

"Music."

"Ah, yes. Lowell sent around a memo prohibiting music in the workplace." Aaron eyed the business dictator in question as he moved around the serving platters the catering staff had just carefully arranged on the buffet. When the man snapped his fingers at one of the servers to get his attention, Aaron looked away. "Lowell said something about the Christmas carols distracting the employees from their work."

"But we're not at the office."

"I'm not sure Lowell sees a distinction. All fun is bad."

"With his lack of holiday spirit, why bother throwing the party at all? Unless he's charging them to attend." Royal's gaze shot to Aaron. "Oh, man. He's not, is he?"

"Worse, I heard the party is in place of year-end bonuses and cost-of-living adjustments for the next year."

"Classy."

Despite his distaste for Lowell, Aaron had to watch over the guy. Aaron had enough troubles without blowing this assignment. Unlike Craft's, Aaron's staff got bonuses and had time off and were even allowed to get sick now and then. All of that required money. Lowell did pay his bills, which allowed Aaron to keep paying his. A timely check was just about the only positive aspect of Lowell's personality Aaron could find.

Not that Lowell was making the current job easy. At the beginning of the assignment, he'd had a habit of disappearing during the middle of the day and then wandering back in with a stupid grin a few hours after lunch. He did that until Aaron started shadowing the older man's every step.

Slim and tall with brown hair peppered with gray, Lowell had the kind of power and money many women found attractive, though Aaron had no idea why. The guy reeked of the same smarminess usually reserved for career politicians. He possessed all the people skills of a serial killer. He never offered his age, but people who knew him back when pegged it in the mid-fifties. He had a wife and a twenty-three-year-old son, and just like the people who worked for him, neither family member could stand him.

Then there was the other side of Lowell's life. The man pretended to be a what-you-see-is-what-you-get type, but Aaron knew better. You couldn't dig into every aspect of a man's existence without having to brush off some dirt. And this Craft guy slid around in mud every single day.

Aaron glanced over at the thirty-something brunette with the long legs and short attention span sitting at the table all alone, sipping on a glass of something clear. "Rumor is Angie requested the party because morale is so low and even in a rough economy she's worried about a mass employee exodus."

"And Lowell sure listens to Angie." Royal half laughed, half coughed. "Speaking of which, it's nice of Lowell to invite the wife and the mistress to the same party."

"Alleged mistress." Aaron said the words as an afterthought as he scanned the room for Mrs. Craft and came up empty. He was just about to send Royal looking for her when the two men waiting by the elevator grabbed his attention.

They had matching military haircuts and dark suits, and neither spent a second checking out the party. They didn't work at Craft. Aaron would put money on that. After the second death threat, he'd run a security check on all employees, past and present. He'd checked out the Elan staff, as well. Either these two slipped through the screening without Aaron noticing—and since one of the guys had shoulders wider than the elevator doors, Aaron doubted it—or they were uninvited. Neither option made Aaron happy.

He elbowed Royal. "Who are those two?"

Royal's gaze followed Aaron's nod. "Waitstaff?"

"Not anyone I checked in."

"And not wearing the right uniform." Royal's gaze narrowed. "Why are they headed for the elevators when the food is in here?"

Royal's shifting to attack mode was all the confirmation Aaron needed of impending trouble. The guy had pitch-perfect instincts thanks to years in and around the mountains of Afghanistan's Kunar Province.

Aaron barked out orders to the rest of the team listening in on the earpieces. "We need help up here. Palmer?"

When Lowell's head of security, Palmer Trask, didn't check in, the emergency signal in Aaron's brain flashed even brighter.

"The lack of a response can't be good," Royal said under his breath.

"We also need to find Craft's wife."

Royal whipped around, his gaze scanning the room. "She was just here."

"Not now." With her model-perfect figure and straight-out-of-a-magazine outfit, the woman stuck out in a crowd even while she hugged the corner of the room. But now Aaron had bigger problems. "I need two people in here. Report to Royal in the dining room. The rest hold the perimeter."

"Do we need to shut the place down?"

Aaron turned to Royal. "Not yet. You stick to Lowell. He doesn't breathe without falling over you."

"Done."

"I'll take the stairs. Let me know where the elevator stops." Aaron did one last visual sweep of the room, looking for other people who failed to trip his memory bank.

"Remember you have two guys to handle when you get up there," Royal said.

Aaron sure as hell hoped the number was only two. "My worry is they are part of a bigger scheme."

"If they are?"

Aaron patted his hip in a weapons check. "I'll handle it."

"Nothing new there."

Chapter Two

Risa Peters clutched her portfolio to her chest and leaned back against the elevator wall. This was the first time she'd chosen a holiday party venue based on a throwaway recommendation during a dinner date with the lawyer she'd seen exactly twice. The same dinner date who failed to call after their last meal together. Since it was already Thursday, she figured the man was on the run, which was a shame because the chocolate-brown hair, blue-green eyes, all-American handsome type appealed to her.

So did the Elan Conference Center. She was only able to book it for an afternoon during the busy season because the place wasn't truly open to the public yet. The center was in the middle of something called a soft opening. The official ribbon cutting would come in mid-January, after the holiday rush subsided. For a discounted fee and an agreement to forgo some party extravagances, Elan agreed to host the party on very little notice.

Risa doubted the office budget at Buchanan Engineering would support the place next year when the amenities hit their stride, but she could enjoy it now. The miles of rolling hills and the long winding drive up to the place sparkled even more in real life than they did on the website. So did the sprawling five-story building with the stone facade and the huge double-door, double-height entry.

It would all work so long as the weather held out. One flake of snow and next week's party would turn into a driving hazard.

Not that any of this—the late planning, the distance or the weather—qualified as being her fault. Oh, no. She'd been the office manager at the engineering firm all of three weeks when she realized the woman who used to have the job, and now held the title of fired former office manager, failed to reserve a place for the annual holiday get-together. Since the engineers liked to party, the oversight bordered on catastrophic. So Risa was here today to scout the center out, see the party room on the fourth floor, then sign the agreement and hand over a check.

If she survived this mess-up, pulled the party off and got all the engineers home without a drunken episode, she'd still have a job next week. And she sure needed the job. Without it she'd never pull herself out of the economic tailspin Paul had thrown her into.

When the elevator doors opened, she almost stepped out of the car. A quick glance at the glowing green number on the panel told her she'd only made it to the third floor. One more to go.

She stepped back just as a beefy hand reached into the open space and jammed the doors before they could close. Two guys with black jackets and broad shoulders slid inside the car. They hugged the front of the elevator, but the walls still closed in on her.

She knew the lights didn't dim at their entry, but everything seemed darker, felt colder, than it had a second before. It was as if the air had been sucked out of the car as they'd moved in.

They didn't look at her. Didn't speak. But the way their combined bodies blocked any chance she might need of a quick exit had her nerves jumping around in her stomach.

She counted the seconds until the car moved again and stopped on the fourth floor. In her head she reached a thousand, but she guessed that was some sort of sick mind trick. Still, when the bell dinged, she shot between them, her hands shoving them apart.

"Excuse me," she said over their surprised grunts.

Then she walked as fast as she could without breaking into an all-out run. A few fast steps and she turned the corner. With her back pressed against the wall, she listened for the two hulks to make sure they didn't follow.

When silence echoed back at her, she inhaled. The sharp smell of paint assailed her nose. A quick glance told her she was alone on a newly constructed floor. Protective paper and painter's tape still covered some of the doors.

"Great." She sucked in as much of the tainted air as she could take in an effort to slow her hammering heart.

Only then did she feel the tiny jabs against her skin. She opened her palms, peeling her fingers away from the tight clench on the leather binder between her shaking hands.

She wasn't the spook-easy type, having learned long ago that some of the most dangerous men in the world didn't lead with their hands or fit into the Neanderthal body type. But she wasn't stupid. Any smart woman would experience a choke of vulnerable panic being trapped alone with those two bruisers on an enclosed elevator.

She walked toward the restroom sign but stopped when she saw the note on the door. Out of Order. Use 5th Floor.

Her residual panic skittered away. Frustration took its place, shaking through her with the force of a runaway truck. It was bad enough the conference manager got stuck on a call and sent her up ahead. Now she had to wander around looking for a restroom.

She glanced at the elevator, then at the emergency stairwell to the left of the bathroom. She'd take her chances on the stairs this time. With terror fueling her steps and wearing a pantsuit and low heels, she could run if she had to. In an elevator, she'd have nowhere to go.

She hit the stairwell and let her pumps click against the cement steps as she traveled up a floor. A quick peek through the small slit where she opened the door showed nothing but a carpeted hallway with an abandoned industrial carpet shampooer against the wall. Most of the doors weren't even on their hinges yet on this floor.

She waited for any sign of life, any noise. When the floor remained quiet, she snuck into the ladies' restroom and let the door softly shut behind her on a swish.

With her palms flat against the fancy quartz sink, she stood still and let her breathing and heart rate dip back into normal range. As she pivoted for the stalls, the main door flew open. A blur dressed in black raced toward her. Before she could scream, hands clamped down on her arms and the figure shoved her hard against a stall door and back into the enclosed area. She only stopped when the back of her legs hit the toilet.

When her brain kicked back into gear, her arms and

legs started moving. Her attacker's hand settled over her mouth even as she shook her head to avoid him.

"Stop. I'm here to help." The harsh whisper bounced off the tiles as the man crowded around her, though his focus was centered on the restroom door.

One more step and her back hit the far stall wall and her head came up. If the guy wanted to hurt her, he'd have to watch her as he did it…and be on the receiving end of the battle of a lifetime.

The air gathered in her lungs and then rushed out in a raging scream as she decided to go for his face. When he turned back to her, her next breath stalled and her brain cells sputtered to a halt. "Aaron?"

"Risa?" His fingers clenched against her skin one last time then his arms dropped to his sides. "What are you doing here?"

"It's a ladies' restroom."

"No, I mean…the building. This area. Why are you here?"

"You told me about this place when I said I needed a party venue. Why are you here?"

"This is unbelievable." His mouth stayed open even after he stopped talking.

His shock was nothing compared to hers. No matter how hard she tried to blink, she couldn't. She took in the same sexy eyes. Same dark brown hair he liked to smooth his hand through. A dark suit and a firm jaw.

But not everything about him looked familiar. She focused on the gun tucked into the holster at his waist. "Since when does a tax attorney carry a gun?"

He held up his hands. "Keep your voice down."

"Are you kidding me?"

"Not at all." His voice barely carried over the soft

hum from the heating vent above her head. "I can explain all of this."

Fury blew over her with the force of a hurricane. "While you're at it, maybe you can make up an excuse for why you didn't call after our last date."

"What?"

"You know, the dinner we had. The call you never made." Her head buzzed with red-hot rage at the memory.

He finally clamped his jaw shut. "This isn't the right time."

"Oh, really?"

He winced the second before he glanced behind him again. "Look, I know this is awkward."

"No kidding." This time she did keep her voice down, but only because she was muttering.

"In my defense, I've been a little busy." His mouth hovered over her ear as he spoke.

"Lying takes up a lot of your time, does it?" Now he had her whispering. And arguing in a bathroom stall on an empty floor of a not-yet-opened building.

The day just kept getting better and better.

"We can fight about this later, which I'm not looking forward to at all, by the way, but right now we have to—" He reached for her again.

"Since when are you so grabby?" She shrugged out of his grasp and then stopped when she spied the tiny lines of tension around his mouth. "What is it?"

"I need you to stay calm."

"I'm not thirteen. I can take bad news." She fought the urge to ruin her point by rolling her eyes.

"Then you won't lose it when I tell you we have to hide."

She tried to stop her eyes from blinking so fast. "I didn't say that."

ANGIE TROUTMAN STOOD up from the empty table without bothering to scan the room. People were staring and whispering because that's what these losers did. So much jealousy packed into one small room. The room pulsed with it. She was almost sorry she'd talked Lowell into wasting money on them. Their lack of gratitude choked out any chance of enjoying the party.

She scanned the unhappy faces for Palmer, official Craft security, but instead spied a member of the outside team hired to back up Palmer. Not that the backup team viewed itself as anything other than being in charge. She'd warned Lowell about the potential turf war and he'd ignored her, citing the death threats.

Men never listened.

She tried for eye contact with the random security guard nearby. She couldn't remember his name. It was something odd, one of those names parents chose when they wanted to be clever but ultimately ended up dooming their children to snickers.

But the name didn't matter. She had a bigger issue. Aaron McBain had been trouble since he'd walked through the Craft lobby doors and taken over without saying a word. Something about his presence demanded attention. He issued orders and people jumped.

Worse, bringing him on board added to the Craft hierarchy, a pyramid she'd already given up so much to climb. After only a few days in the building, McBain had showed up everywhere, making it nearly impossible for her to speak privately with Lowell when needed. And now, when she needed him to stay in one place and in clear sight, McBain had disappeared off the floor. Hardly the keen skills of a crack security expert promised by the lucrative contract he'd signed with Craft.

Since his assistant—whatever his name was—was

talking to someone rather than looking at her, she poked him in the arm to get his attention. "What's your name?"

His head turned toward her, his gaze bouncing down to her hand and then back to her face, but his frown never wavering. "It's still Royal Jenkins, ma'am. Just like it was when you asked yesterday."

She'd insist on his company firing him from this assignment if she had the power to do so, and by Monday she'd convince Lowell to give it to her. She'd see if this man's voice still dripped with disdain when he was standing in front of her desk, begging for his job. "Well, Roy. We have a—"

"Royal."

As if she had time for this holier-than-thou male nonsense. She let her fake smile fall. "Where is your boss?"

"Excuse me?"

"McBain. His job is to watch Mr. Craft." She glanced to where Lowell last stood and froze when she saw him across the room, handing his wife a drink. With a quick mental shake, Angie returned to the crisis at hand.

"He's checking the rest of the building."

She felt the blood drain from her head. "I don't pay him to be hotel security."

"Craft pays for his expertise. Right now he is ensuring the safety and integrity of the floors above us, which is protocol."

That was the last place he could be at that moment. She couldn't have him snooping around. "I need him here."

Royal's eyes narrowed. "Why?"

She inhaled deeply, trying to calm the sudden swirl of rage and anxiety inside her. If she showed any outward sign of concern, this man would jump on it. He might be insubordinate, but he wasn't stupid. She knew that from the way his gaze wandered around the room, taking in every movement, assessing and analyzing.

She folded her fingers together in front of her. "McBain has declared himself in charge of Mr. Craft's personal safety. As such, your man should be in sight of Mr. Craft at all times."

The stern line of Royal's mouth eased. "I appreciate your…unique concern for Mr. Craft."

"Excuse me?" Her voice turned to ice.

Royal didn't even flinch. Certainly didn't back off. "You are invested in your boss. I understand that."

She had to clench her jaw to keep from screaming. All men were the same. They led with their pants, but she did not have the time to charm this one, so she let the fury bubbling inside her erupt into a heated whisper. "Call McBain now. I want him in front of me within the next two minutes."

"I'll let him know you requested to talk with him." Royal nodded, then turned slightly, giving her his back as he motioned for one of his men to step forward.

Angie ignored the sharp dismissal. Roy or whatever his name was would learn the hard way not to cross her. She would make it her mission to put him in the unemployment office.

But not today. She was too busy staring past him to the elevator bank. The red light held on number five, exactly where it was supposed to be, yet she knew in her soul something was deeply wrong.

Chapter Three

Aaron's bad day tripped and fell right into nightmare territory. He stared at the woman he'd last seen across the table at an Italian restaurant. Same honey-brown hair. Pretty face, intelligent dark eyes. Only this time the smile had been replaced with flat-lined lips. Wariness and more than a touch of female indignation now played across her face.

Risa clearly thought their biggest problem was his late post-date call. Little did she know that was flowers and chocolates territory compared to what they were facing now.

He thought about reaching for her but decided to hold up his hands instead since she looked about two seconds away from hitting something, namely him. "Listen to me."

She crossed her arms over her stomach until every muscle in her body practically dared him to make another mistake. "Go ahead."

He waded in even though he knew the smartest thing was to knock her out with the gentlest tap possible, drag her out the door and rush her to safety. But if his dating etiquette ticked her off, he could only guess how she'd react to a physical solution to their current problem.

He'd already dumped a few sins at her feet. Lying

to her had seemed like the safest bet at the time. Now not so much.

Then there was the problem of Royal listening in through their private communication circuit. He'd ride Aaron about the date-gone-wrong for years unless Aaron took the focus off the personal conversation and put it back on the mess swirling around them.

"Not a word." He whispered the command and knew Royal understood when he chuckled over the comm, then mumbled something about Angie wanting him. Right, as if that woman was even on his radar at the moment. "Silence."

Risa's eyebrow shot up in a perfect angry teacher glare. "Did you just tell me to shut up?"

"Definitely not." Hard to explain he was talking to the guy at the other end of a listening device. Better to look like a total jerk than expose every aspect of the operation at this tenuous stage. "I specifically did not use those words. I'm not a total idiot."

"Really?"

It was time to calm the situation down before she went into ballistic mode. Aaron went with the simple truth. "It's dangerous here."

"In the bathroom?"

"You need to see the bigger picture here."

She exhaled in that you-are-annoying way women telegraphed so well. "I have no idea what that means."

"The danger is in every inch of this building."

"This is the strangest excuse for a noncall ever. If you didn't want to go out again, you could have just said—" Her words cut off at the sound of the sharp whack against the outside wall.

One of his hands went to her mouth, and the other cradled her head from behind. "Quiet."

This time she followed his direction. Her big eyes popped open even wider as she nodded.

"Someone is out there." He stalled by stating the obvious. It gave his mind a second to run through the memory of the building's floor plans.

She held up two fingers.

"What?" He eased his hand away from her mouth.

Her bottom lip trembled. Other than that, her mouth barely moved as she whispered, "They're huge."

"What are we talking about?"

"On the elevator. Two men and they're big. Like the size of a small shed. And pretty scary. Did I mention that?"

Tension rolled across his shoulders and cramped the nerve at the back of his neck. "Did they threaten you?"

"Didn't say a word. Didn't really have to. These guys are imposing. I'm thinking any woman alone and without a gun or a massive boyfriend would run."

Aaron's muscles unclenched but not much. He still had to hope the two she described were the same two guys he'd been following and not a second muscle team. "I need to get you out of here."

"There's a stairwell."

Her skin had paled to the hue of crisp white sheets. Every few seconds a fine tremble moved through her body and vibrated under his hand. He knew she had to be terrified, but she didn't curl into a ball or so much as whimper. He found that strength more attractive than her long legs and sexy smile, though those sure were impressive.

The twinge of guilt over not calling her back as promised, as he had intended to do before work kicked up and pounded him, turned into a crashing wave. Any man would be lucky to get another date with her and he'd blown the chance. The least he could do was get her out of the building while he figured out the threat level.

"Stay here." He eased away from her and slipped across the floor in soundless steps. "Royal?"

When Aaron didn't get a reply, he tapped on the earpiece. He'd just reached the door when it slammed open and into him. The force shoved him back against the wall. His gun jerked from his fingers and clanked against the tile floor by his feet.

The doorknob jabbed into his midsection as he bit back a curse. One of the men he'd seen from the elevator shoved his weight against the door, banging on his thick body until Aaron thought his chest would cave in. The move stole his breath, trapping his hands in front of him and pinning his back to the wall.

He shifted and shoved, trying to get traction and a better grip, but the metal door crushed his gut, and his strength proved useless. Blackness raged through his veins as his gaze bounced between the vulnerable woman frozen in place in the middle of the room and the muscle trying to knock him unconscious with a door.

The sudden roar of Royal's voice echoed in Aaron's ears, but he couldn't make out the words. All Aaron heard was the rush of his own breath as it moved through him. His brain scrambled for a backup plan.

"Double up." It was their code for assistance, but Aaron wasn't even sure he said the words out loud. The doorknob connected with his gut once again and knocked the air right out of his lungs.

The attacker's friend moved into the room, his shoes quiet against the floor but his shoulders knocking against the door frame. Risa hadn't exaggerated. He had a thick neck and biceps that kept his arms from lying close to his side. From this distance, it was clear the guy engaged in some serious training. The type that included flipping tractor tires. This guy obviously was in charge.

The man didn't even spare Aaron a glance. He aimed the gun directly at Risa's head. "Enough."

Aaron blinked, knowing he was the intended recipient of that message. "What do you want?"

"Her."

"Me?" Risa squealed the question, her voice bouncing off the walls.

The attacker held out a beefy hand in Risa's direction. "Time to go, Angie."

Risa's fingers tightened on the edge of the stall door until her knuckles turned white. "I don't—"

Her gaze raced to Aaron's face. He nodded, letting her know she could answer. The longer they dragged this out, the better chance Royal could burst in with reinforcements.

Risa swallowed hard enough for her throat to move. "Who's Angie?"

The leader shook his head as he took a step in her direction. "We're not doing this."

"You have the wrong woman."

"And you've wasted enough of my time."

Risa shook her head, her bewilderment obvious in every part of her body and in her voice. "What is happening here?"

"You don't get to ask questions." The leader pointed at Risa before sparing Aaron a glance. "Who are you?"

"I work at Craft. The lady and I met at the party downstairs and came up here for some privacy." Aaron went for a guy-to-guy moment but knew he'd misfired when a feral smile spread across the leader's face.

The guy took his time on a visual tour of Risa's body. "Nice."

The attacker crowded against the door barked out a laugh as Risa's face morphed from white to gray. These two made quite a team. The type that reinforced Aaron's belief in women's self-defense classes.

"Come here." The leader reached for her as he made his demand.

Just as fast, Risa stepped back. Her heels clicked against the floor as she scooted her body deeper into the stall.

"Stop." The leader lunged and grabbed her elbow. With one tug, he had her back in the middle of the room and within inches of the gun in his other hand.

"You have the wrong person." Her words rushed out.

"Let's all step back and relax for a second." Aaron shifted his weight as he spoke. He eased one foot out from behind the door.

"Shut up," the attacker who was crushing him shouted.

Risa shook her head. "We didn't do anything."

"You are on this floor, right where you're supposed to be." When the attacker pulled on her arm, she stumbled. "Move again without permission and I'll put a bullet in your boyfriend."

The man made the threat, but both men's guns never wavered. Both pointed at Risa, which gave Aaron the advantage he needed.

With as little movement as possible, he slid his hand into his inside jacket pocket, fumbling with the fabric until his fingers connected with the metal from one of his extra weapons.

Using all his weight, he crashed his body against the door and knocked the backup attacker off balance. His head snapped back when the door connected with his face. Blood spurted from his nose, and his hands went to his face as his attention slipped from the attack.

"Risa, get down!" Aaron barely got the words out before the leader turned toward him.

She dropped to her knees as the room broke into chaos. Aaron got off two quick rounds that boomed through the shouting. One shot exploded through the door, catching the backup attacker in the side and sending him falling back into the hallway on a howl of pain.

Aaron's second shot slammed into the leader's shoulder and spun him around and straight into Risa. He stumbled over her, then fell to the floor over her back.

Despite Royal's yelling in his ear and Risa's screaming in the small room, Aaron kept moving. He pocketed the fallen attacker's dropped weapon. With a quick glance at the man heaving and rolling in pain in the hall, Aaron raced toward Risa. He reached down and pulled her up beside him, then pivoted toward freedom.

They got two steps before her trim body turned to deadweight. It was as if her feet fell out from under her. Aaron assumed she tripped and bent down to lift her, only then seeing the death grip the leader had on her ankle.

"Drop the gun." He issued the order through shallow breaths.

As he held the weapon pointed at them, the man's hand shook. He blinked repeatedly as if trying to keep a cloud from settling over his mind.

Aaron didn't waste any time. He kicked out, ramming his heel into the other man's fist and sending the gun flying from his loose fingers. The second kick landed on the guy's temple and pressed him into an unconscious heap.

Risa gasped as she lost her balance and Aaron grabbed her. Relief flooded through him when her hand tightened on his. With a tug, he drew her into his arms and held on with all his strength.

Feeling her body shake against his brought reality rushing back. She was a civilian in the wrong place at the very wrong time. She was innocent, as were the people downstairs. Someone was making a move on Lowell and somehow mistook Risa for Angie. The plan reeked of desperation and poor planning. That meant everyone was a target and no one in the building was safe.

Royal's voice finally registered in Aaron's ear. Instead of answering, he asked a question of his own. "Where are you?"

"Coming." A one-word reply, and then silence filled the other end of the line.

"Royal?"

Risa wrapped her fingers around Aaron's arm. "What's wrong?"

"I'm not sure." It was as if the world went quiet. No one even breathed on the other end of the comm.

Worry for his team warred with the fury racing through his body over the attack on Risa and how close he came to having her pulled out of his hands. But the groan in the hallway as the slumped man tried to sit up against the wall refocused Aaron's attention on the disaster on this floor.

"Stay here." He tried to move away from Risa, but she held on.

"No way are you walking away from me again."

Since she left his shooting hand free, he didn't argue. With her body plastered against his side, he walked toward the injured man.

"Who do you work for?"

The man on the floor snarled as he pressed his hand against his bloody side. His shoulders rose and fell on labored breaths, but he had enough energy left to pronounce his loyalty. "Go to hell."

Aaron shoved his foot against the man's open wound and the blood-soaked shirt underneath. The string of curses started a second later, but Aaron didn't let up. He increased the pressure until the other man squirmed against the floor.

He winced and swore. "I don't know."

Aaron leaned in, letting menace flow through his voice as he aimed his gun at the attacker's head. "Someone is paying you and you have two seconds to tell me."

The guy slid flat against the floor, his voice shifting from talking to panting. "My orders were to grab the woman."

Risa leaned over his shoulder. "You picked the wrong one."

Confusion wrinkled the man's brow.

Aaron didn't let that part of the conversation go any further. "I want a name."

"I don't know." The man shouted his answer this time.

Fearing the guy had an earpiece or a mic, Aaron ended the interrogation. With a sweep of his arm, he landed a sleeping blow to the side of the guy's head, knocking him unconscious.

"He's still bleeding," she said.

"Right." Part of him didn't mind the idea of this guy bleeding out, not after what he'd tried to do to Risa, but Aaron figured he'd lost enough humanity in this job. He couldn't afford much more.

Using the cloth towels on the sink top, he constructed

a makeshift bandage and pressed it hard to the guy's side, anchoring it there with his belt.

Risa leaned over Aaron's shoulder. "Will that be enough?"

He didn't pretend to be a medical expert, but he knew the guy needed real attention soon. "For now."

After a quick check for more weapons and a phone, which proved futuile, Aaron turned back to Risa, expecting to see fear or disgust at the violence and bloodshed. Instead, she bit her lower lip, as if in deep thought.

"What is going on? I came to check out a party venue and walked into some sort of mistaken-identity nightmare." Her voice slowly returned to normal as she spoke. Gone was the tremor of fear. In its place was a simple determination to get through the next few minutes.

Aaron appreciated the change, and the bluntness of her response startled him into an honest answer. "It looks like someone is planning an attack against the businessman downstairs and is using a woman to get to him."

"This Angie person."

"Yes, and I have no idea how anyone would confuse the two of you." Aaron's mind shifted to the Lowell's mistress. They both had long brown hair and hovered around five foot six. But the similarities stopped there.

Angie was in her early thirties, a few years older than Risa, with a deep bourbon-soaked voice and a buxom Barbie Doll shape that had men discounting her brains. Aaron didn't like the overly done look, but he never underestimated her. The woman ran the office with a quiet confidence and manipulated everyone in it, ignoring the affair whispers blowing around her.

Where Angie reminded Aaron of smoke-filled back rooms and expensive jewelry tastes, Risa…glowed.

With the soft skin and shiny hair, it was as if sunshine kept her in its sights. The skeptic in him wondered if he'd seen so much bad that goodness of any type got magnified to an unrealistic degree.

His luck with women usually made sure that didn't happen. One broken engagement hadn't ruined him for all women, but it did make him wary. But he'd been struck by Risa from the very first time he saw her fighting with her laptop in a coffee shop a few weeks ago. Wearing sweatpants and a slim T-shirt, she'd had that sexy, ruffled, just-out-of-bed look that had sent his temperature spiking.

She didn't have to work very hard at being pretty. When you turned over on the mattress in the morning, you knew who you'd see on the pillow beside you. She wouldn't have to put on her face first. At least that's how it had worked in Aaron's mind. He'd never gotten as far as the bed, or even the couch, let alone a kiss, with Risa.

Yet.

Risa treated him to a half smile. "You know when I see this Angie person and do a comparison, you might get punched for that comment, right?"

"I'd prefer you anytime and anywhere." He held a hand up as a pledge. "Couldn't be more serious about that."

Risa lifted an eyebrow but didn't respond to that. "Why are these two up here? It's supposed to be closed off."

"Good question." He put his hands on her upper arms and with as little pressure as possible, moved her until she stood near the opening to the room with her back against the wall. "Stay right there."

"Where else would I go?"

She sounded almost exasperated with his suggestion. She did everything but snort. He had to smile at her spunk. She'd been manhandled and threatened, seen men shot and attacked. Still, she stood there and handled it all. Not bad for a woman who sat behind a desk all day.

Aaron dragged the attacker by his ankles from the hallway and dropped his body next to his partner by the stall. After a check of the leader's pockets, Aaron unloaded the weapons, littering the floor, pocketing the all the ammunition and dumping the guns in the toilet. He kept the leader's secondary gun in case he needed an extra.

He had one last problem as he glanced up at Risa. "Any chance you have any rope?"

She lifted her arms. "Not on me."

"Thought it was worth a shot."

"There are cables and those sorts of things around as part of the construction."

That meant a trip around the building looking for supplies. He doubted they had that sort of time, not when Royal had gone silent. "We'll block the door and trust they'll be out long enough for us to get downstairs and out of the building."

"And if not?"

He stood in front of her, his gaze locked on hers. "I can't be that unlucky."

"You're saying that as a tax attorney, of course."

He didn't try to hide the wince. He'd hoped he'd have another few minutes before the need for an explanation caught up and smacked him in the face. "What makes you think I'm not a lawyer?"

She eyed his hand. "The gun."

"I can explain."

Her head dropped to the side. "Are you going to?"

"Not right now."

"Normally I'd insist, but since I want to leave this place right now—ten minutes ago, actually—we can save the I-lied-to-you-about-everything conversation for later."

Not exactly a bullet dodged. "I'm not really looking forward to that."

"Imagine how I feel."

"Good point."

Chapter Four

Risa slipped into the hallway behind Aaron, never easing up on her double-fisted grip on his jacket. This close, pressed against his back, she felt a subtle minty scent tingle her senses and block out the smell of new paint. She leaned in, almost touching her nose to his rich brown hair, and drew in a hint of his shampoo. Fresh, clean and nonfussy.

Until he showed up waving a gun around, she'd viewed him as uncomplicated and easy. When he'd dropped into the seat across from her at the coffee shop that day they first met, she'd found him to be handsome and smart, with an open smile that lit up his face.

She loved his slightly crooked nose, which he explained got banged up in a college lacrosse game. During their dinner dates, he'd wait until dessert and then slip his hand into hers. Leaving the restaurant, he'd press his palm against the sensitive small of her back. But at every point she thought he'd move their relationship forward, he pulled back.

She'd started to wonder if the attraction only sparked one way. Now she knew something much bigger was going on. He had a secret life. Since she needed his protection and the gun he seemed to handle so well, she didn't hold his other life against him at the moment. There would be time for that later…she hoped.

"Risa?"

"Yes?" She matched her whisper to his as the bathroom door slipped shut behind her.

"I can't breathe."

"What?"

He reached around and touched his fingers to hers. It wasn't until that minute she realized she'd pulled his jacket and dress shirt so tightly that the collar was choking him. His skin turned red and puckered from the force of her grip.

She dropped her hands and stepped back. "I'm so sorry."

He winked at her over his shoulder. "You are more than welcome to undress me later. For now, I need the clothes on and in place."

Then he was off. He eased all six feet of his lean body to the edge of the hallway where it dumped into the larger open space. Bending down, he grabbed something on the floor of the other room and stood back up. When he faced her again, he had a broom in his hands.

Her mind was stuck on repeat. "You've never said anything like that before."

His face went blank. "What are you talking about?"

"Undressing. Sex. Anything intimate."

She thought she saw a smile cross his lips as he brushed past her. A clanking thud echoed down the hall as he jammed the broom in the door handle. Shoving the small phone table outside the bathroom against the door produced a squeak that broke the remaining silence.

The scene took two seconds and amounted to less than a few sounds and a rattle of drawers in the table, and she spent the entire time standing there, staring at his hands and wondering not for the first time what he could do with them. When she blinked, he was in front of her again.

"Did you really think I never had that on my mind? That I never wrestled with the best way to get you out of your clothes?"

"I thought you were a tax attorney."

This time he didn't hide the smile. "I'm pretty sure they appreciate pretty women just as much as other men do."

Okay, not her brightest comment. She'd admit that. Or she would if she could. Something about this conversation made her mind turn to mush. "Well, yeah, I…"

"I'd bet attorneys like sex, too."

She had no idea what to say to that. Luckily, she was spared coming up with something smooth or even coherent, when he held out his hand. She took it without thinking.

"We're going to stand over here, away from this door, and check in with downstairs," he said.

She hated just about every part of the plan. "I thought we were leaving."

"We need to make sure it's clear first. That we aren't in some sort of lockdown." His eyes swept over the sterile surroundings and kept moving as he talked. He checked all around them, as if attackers could come from any angle.

"This is ridiculous. I was just trying to book a party." She rubbed her forehead as she muttered.

When his fingers brushed over hers and he brought her hand to his mouth, her breath caught in her chest. Just rumbled up and stuck there.

"It's going to be okay." He leaned in and touched his warm lips against her forehead.

She would have said something if she could have forced even a syllable out. Instead, the words lodged in her throat, right next to her last breath. Much more of this tug of emotions, this wobbling between fear and attraction, and she'd pass out.

With his gaze locked on hers, he let go of her hand and tapped his ear and began speaking. "Royal."

"Is that code for something?" she whispered.

"It's a name." Aaron tried two more times, then frowned.

She didn't need a law degree or a gun license to know the lack of a response was a very bad thing. "What's wrong?"

"Nothing." His forced smile said the opposite.

With a hand on her stomach he pressed her back against the wall and lifted his gun as he approached the emergency door. The stance was sure, as if refined from years of law enforcement or security experience.

A flash of a memory hit her. The first time he held her hand, his strength surprised her. She now wondered if he'd ever spent a workday behind a desk.

As he reached for the doorknob, she felt a whoosh of air behind her. An elbow clamped around her throat, and the hard end of a gun pressed against her temple before she could cry out for help.

But she didn't need to. Aaron had turned and now had his weapon trained on whoever held her.

The look of burning fury in his eyes turned them from green-blue to the deep, cold hue of the ocean. He didn't look her in the eye. All his focus centered on the face hovering just out of her line of sight.

Her heart slammed hard enough inside her to hit the base of her throat. She would have fallen to the floor if the stranglehold on her hadn't kept her upright. Between the roar of blood to her ears and the sudden buzzing in her head, she could barely hear.

"Let the lady go." Aaron's flat voice rang throughout the unfinished floor.

The man's heavy breathing hit her cheek as he spoke. "This is not the time for you to be a hero."

She totally disagreed and wanted to scream that fact, but she used all of her energy to stay still instead. Aaron had been playing the role of hero since he'd stormed into the bathroom to warn her. She would let him play it forever if he somehow got them out of this nightmare.

When she finally forced her body to breathe and her heart to pump in the nonstroke range, she picked up the sounds of the room. The uncovered lights hummed above her head, and the floor creaked beneath her feet as she shifted her weight.

"You know something?" Aaron slipped a second gun out of his jacket pocket and fixed that one on the attacker, too. "I'm getting tired of guys grabbing her."

"I don't know anything about that."

"You're number three and I'm about out of patience."

The man's hold tightened. "She's coming with me."

Risa grabbed on to the arm choking her, hoping to push him off, but the thick muscle didn't give. The attacker tucked her body against his like a shield. She feared any bullet would travel through her before ever reaching him.

Even with Aaron's skill and laserlike focus, he couldn't make a bullet's trajectory bend and sweep. This wasn't a movie. This was real life, and the possibility of her bleeding out on the floor grew greater with each passing second.

Her attacker's chest expanded against her back right

before he spoke. "I have her, so you're going to step back."

"And I have a bullet just begging for you to move one inch closer to the edge of stupid."

Fear had her teeth chattering and the blood pounding in her temples. "Aaron."

"Yeah. Listen to the lady, Aaron." The attacker gathered her even closer until his hair brushed against her cheek. "You've got her scared. I can feel her shaking, and it doesn't have to be this way."

"Why do you want her?"

"I don't care about her."

Not the first time she'd heard those words. But she'd never faced dismissal at the end of a gun. Lied to, dumped? Yes. Threatened? Never in her life until the past few hours.

"So this is about money," Aaron said, the disgust filling his voice.

"Isn't everything?" The attacker motioned with his gun. "Move to the side."

When Aaron obeyed, her heart dropped to her knees. They'd barely gone out, but she expected him to help… to do something before just handing her over. She tried to wrap her brain around what she thought she'd learned about him today and what was happening now. He'd rescued her in the bathroom. Abandoning her now without a fight made no sense.

"I need your gun on the floor. All of them. Even the ones I can't see." The attacker pivoted as he spoke, keeping her angled in front of him and between him and the potential exchange of fire.

Aaron's knees bent and his hands started toward the floor. She wanted to shout and beg. She went for attack mode instead. A smart woman didn't wait to be rescued.

She could kick out, maybe hit this guy at a vulnerable spot and give Aaron a minute to get off a shot. She'd just decided to launch when his furious gaze caught hers. With an almost imperceptible shake of his head, he had her mind spinning in confusion.

"That's it." Her attacker braced his legs apart as he spoke. "You do the right thing here, Aaron, and we all go home."

"Except me." She knew that truth as sure as she knew anything.

The man chuckled. "I'm afraid someone has plans for you."

"Who?" Aaron asked.

"Put the weapons down." All amusement was wiped clear of the man's voice. He was back to waving the gun around and promising pain without ever saying it.

This time, Aaron didn't stall his movements. One gun clicked against the floor. The second one almost touched and then Aaron whipped it back up and shot at the attacker's legs. The weapon fired and the shot boomed through the room.

Risa closed her eyes waiting to feel the sting of a bullet or have the man drop behind her, but nothing happened. Her attacker didn't even flinch.

He chose to break into a full-belly laugh. "You missed."

Aaron fired again, but nothing happened after the initial crack of the weapon.

"Guess it's my turn." The attacker's finger moved on the trigger.

She screamed for Aaron to duck as she shoved her elbow against her attacker's midsection with all her strength. Every cell, every muscle. All of her weight centered on unbalancing the man before he could take them down.

Everything happened at the same time. Aaron dove for her legs as the door to the stairs slammed open. She could hear him telling her to drop on top of him as a man filled the doorway and came into the hallway firing.

One minute she stood locked against her attacker's body even as she struggled to slip out of his grip. The next a huge weight fell from behind her, nearly taking her slamming to the floor with him.

Aaron tugged her down, then wrapped his arms around her waist and took her with him in a diving roll. Her body slid under his as the room passed by her in a blurry haze. Gunfire exploded and a light shattered somewhere behind her. By the time the room stopped spinning she'd heard a roar of fury and a thud.

When she opened her eyes again, the attacker lay a few feet ahead with blood trickling from his forehead. Shock rolled over her until all she could do was stare. Violence on television, where actors got hit, fell and the action cut to commercial, didn't compare to the real-life version where people rolled around bleeding.

Seeing someone die right at her feet elicited horror, pain, anxiety. But as she sat there, the overwhelming reaction was shock. The tips of her fingers tingled as the last of the feelings left her body.

A man in a suit loomed above them. Twenty-something, blond and lethal. His gun stayed aimed and his frown locked on Aaron.

She was done being a victim. Done with rotten luck. Bad karma, or whatever had been kicking her around for the past year, could go find someone else to stalk.

Starting now. She scrambled to sit up, reaching for one of the guns.

Aaron caught her in midlunge. "Whoa. This guy's with us."

The blond dropped his weapon to his side as the corner of his mouth lifted in a smile. "How the hell did you miss from that distance?"

"That's just it. I didn't." The grumble in Aaron's voice sounded huskier than usual.

"Okay, now I'm confused. I have no idea what you're talking about." She knew that was the understatement of the century, but she said the words anyway.

Aaron sat up and studied the gun he'd used. "This is the one I picked up from the other attacker. It's loaded with dummy cartridges."

"What?" The blond reached down and grabbed it. "Why would that be?"

"I have no idea. It doesn't make sense. Who tries to kidnap a woman using fake ammo?" Aaron stood up and with a light touch, brought her to her feet beside him. "Are you okay?"

She couldn't believe her legs held her. The sudden softness in his voice did nothing to calm the nerves that began jumping around inside her. "Speaking as the almost-kidnapped victim, no."

When she looked up, both men were staring at her.

The blond man's attention soon shifted to Aaron. "Any idea why she's the target?"

"Angie is."

"That's just as confusing. I'd think anyone who wanted Angie hurt is downstairs." The blond turned back to Risa. "Were you hit?"

She inhaled several times, trying to ease the anxiety flowing through her. Much more unwanted excitement and she'd need a hospital and a vacation from a job she hadn't had long enough to earn time off.

As oxygen returned to her lungs and blood fueled her brain, some of the more obvious pieces fell together. "I'm guessing you're Royal?"

The big man smiled and held out his hand. "Yes, ma'am. Royal Jenkins."

If he felt the tremors shaking through her, he was nice enough not to show it. "I'm Risa and thanks for arriving when you did."

Royal nodded at Aaron. "He guided me in."

"How?" She'd been in that room, heard everything and had no idea reinforcements hid on the stairs ready to pounce. She didn't want to think about the years of life she'd lost thanks to unnecessary panic.

"I told him I was coming and then I waited and listened in." Royal tapped on his ear. "He dropped clues."

Aaron's exhale was loud enough to drown out part of the conversation. His fingers slid under her elbow. "Risa, answer the question."

The burst of anger surprised her. "Which one?"

His gaze roamed over her, not in a heated way. In a ready-to-tie-her-down-and-amputate-a-leg way if he had to. "Are you hurt?"

The answer for his sharp change in personality hit her hard enough to make her stumble. Concern. She'd doubted him for a second, but his determination to see her safe really had never wavered.

A trickle of guilt washed over her. "No, just stunned."

"Getting yelled at probably isn't helping," Royal mumbled as he looked first to the left and then to the right, anywhere but at Aaron.

"At the moment, I'm more concerned with keeping her alive than sparing her feelings," Aaron returned.

"Apparently."

Male grumbling wasn't making the tense situation any easier. She needed them both focused on finding an answer. "Can someone tell me why this keeps happening? Why does someone want Angie? Why do they think I'm her? I don't get any of it."

"I wish I knew an answer to even one of those questions." Aaron shook his head as he turned to Royal. "What's going on downstairs?"

"It was under control when I left, but then I saw your guy on the stairs and followed."

Another lightbulb flickered to life in her brain. "Which is why you went silent when Aaron tried to reach you earlier. You didn't want him to hear you."

"Nice." Royal drug out the word nice and long, using more syllables than there were letters in the word, as he nodded in obvious appreciation. "I like smart women."

Aaron grabbed his gun off the floor. "Why do you think I'm dating her?"

Royal's eyebrow kicked up. "You are?"

Risa struggled to hide her reaction. It took all of her concentration not to let her jaw drop. Ignoring the lightness dancing in her stomach at his words wasn't easy, either. This wasn't the place or the time, but…well, she wasn't dead yet.

Rather than make some big declaration, Aaron shrugged.

Disappointment rolled through her. "That's your answer to your friend's question?"

"He's my assistant," Aaron corrected her. When she broke eye contact, he put a hand on her arm and drew her gaze back. "And admittedly this hasn't been our best date, but the next one will be better."

She stared at him for a second, not saying anything,

just enjoying the idea of any future outside this room, away from this building. "Promise me it won't happen at Elan and I'll think about saying yes."

Chapter Five

Lowell followed his son, Brandon, into the small room down the hall from the holiday party. The internal space didn't have a window or any witnesses, which Lowell assumed was the point. Brandon always did have a sense of the dramatic.

Since arriving, Brandon had stood in the corner of the party room huddled with his mother. Together they'd nearly blended into the Christmas tree. They certainly hadn't mingled or helped with any of the necessary social niceties of this type of event. Hell, getting them to even show up to present a united family front had taken a threat from him.

Never mind the pressure he was under. Never mind the threats against his life.

Lowell blamed his wife for the untenable situation. Despite all his efforts, she'd raised a spoiled and oversensitive heir who frequently ran low on common sense. She'd had one task in her entire adult life—parenting a son—and she'd blown it as she did everything else.

Oh, Lowell had tried to step in, but attempts to toughen Brandon up had backfired. An overpriced therapist and a coddling mother undermined every tiny shuffle forward. Which was why Brandon failed at everything he tried.

Wanting this part of the evening over so that he could concentrate on some more interesting entertainment, Lowell agreed to listen. He walked to the small conference room table in the center of the room and leaned against it with his arms folded across his chest. The stance said *make it quick* and Brandon had better comply.

"What is so important?" Lowell's disinterested exhale skipped across the room.

"How could you bring her here?" Brandon's blue eyes flashed with fire as his hands clenched and unclenched beside him.

So dramatic. "First, lower your voice. I am your father and I will have your respect. We both know I've earned it."

"Mother left."

Ah, yes. Sonya, the original drama queen. "When?"

"Do you even care?"

"She promised she would be here." Not that Lowell minded at this point. She'd come in, posed for a photo and hadn't caused a scene. These days that was as good as he could expect from Sonya. Probably meant she was overmedicating again.

Besides, with her gone he was not obligated to play the role of dutiful husband. That game wore thin fast, as did her crying jags.

"She got in the car five minutes ago. You didn't even see her leave the room." Brandon's chest rose and fell on heavy breaths.

Much more of this and the boy would whip himself into a full-fledged rage. Lowell was not in the mood for the useless burst of emotion.

"She was humiliated. You set her up to be a joke."

Brandon took a step forward, actually looked as if he might lunge.

Lowell's scowl stopped the attempt, but he suspected stopping the nonsense would take a bit longer. "I have expended a great deal of money on private school, tutors and college to teach you manners. You've had a DUI disappear. Your college trouble with a forged paper went away without you ever stepping in front of a disciplinary board."

"I didn't ask for any of that."

"Now would be a good time to show some gratitude for all this family has done for you." The need to lecture never stopped. Brandon was determined to tarnish the family name, and Lowell had grown weary of the childish outbursts.

"I am twenty-three."

"Then stop acting like a petulant child." Lowell glanced at his watch. The five minutes he'd allotted for this sideshow was almost over.

Brandon either missed the not-so-subtle message or ignored it. "You put your wife and your mistress in the same room."

Heat raced through Lowell's veins. "That's enough."

"She was fidgeting and couldn't hold her head up." Brandon took to the topic now. His face flushed and his hands flew through the air as he talked. "What did you think would happen? Everyone was whispering. It's bad enough you do that behind Mom's back, while you're sleeping around at the office, but to have it thrown in her face—"

"I said enough." The boy just kept pushing. All that festering disappointment at who Brandon had become rushed up, threatening to explode.

But Lowell refused to give Brandon that satisfaction. As a boy he'd tried to goad and inflame. Everything would settle down in Lowell's life with Sonya, and then Brandon would create some new problem, cause some new conflict that had to be solved and send the family spinning again. Lowell was done feeding that particular monster.

"This is not your business, Brandon."

"She's my mother."

"And my wife. I will deal with her. I am sure this was nothing more than the onset of one of her usual headaches." Only his wife would view living with every luxury in a three-story museum of a house she decorated herself as some sort of prison.

"I told her to go home."

The boy never stopped. "What is your game here, Brandon? Still running to Mommy when Daddy won't let you get your way? I didn't say yes to you last week, so you are using your mother and her weaknesses to your advantage."

"I asked you for a simple job." Brandon's breathing had kicked up until every part of his body vibrated as he talked.

"And I told you no. I don't engage in nepotism. I earned my way and you can, too. Frankly, it's long past time you grew up." Lowell was not going to relive this conversation. He'd made his decision. He took two steps toward the door in a silent declaration that the conversation had ended.

"That is why I asked for the job."

He stopped and glanced at the young man he'd once hoped would followed him into the family business, and realized that dream had died long ago. "No, you asked because you've burned every other bridge. You lost your first job out of college because you were ignorant. I told you never to use your real name on the internet. You should have listened to me, but you didn't. Well, Brandon, lesson learned."

"I know the only one you like to help around here is Angie—"

"You will refer to her as Ms. Troutman and you will be respectful. She is a trusted member of my team."

Brandon laughed. "Is that what we're calling it these days?"

Behind the tough talk Lowell saw his son's wariness. Realizing this was all false bravado stopped Lowell from kicking the kid out. "If you are trying to convince me you're growing up, you are failing miserably."

After a light knock, the door opened. Security chief Palmer Trask slipped inside, his eyes going between the two men. "Excuse me, sir."

"Come in." Lowell waved him in, more than happy to end the family discussion. "Brandon and I are done talking."

Palmer nodded. "Yes, sir."

"Where have you been? And while you're at it, explain why all the so-called security professionals to whom I pay huge fees can't seem to be bothered to actually protect anything or anyone."

"Sir, we have a problem."

"I believe that was my point."

Palmer cleared his voice. "There may be an issue that requires some delicacy."

Since Brandon just stood there, Lowell decided the best recourse was to talk around him. "Pretend he's not here and be more specific."

Palmer linked his fingers behind his back and rocked back on his heels. "I haven't seen McBain or his second-in-command in quite some time. They went upstairs to check on an issue and I've lost radio communication. He has a cell, but I can't get through."

From his dealings with McBain, Lowell knew the man took his job seriously. He wouldn't leave his post without cause. "We need to check the conference center while the party continues."

"Is that safe?" Brandon asked.

"This is all precaution. I'm sure everything is fine." Lowell spared Brandon a glance before returning his attention to Palmer. "As quietly as possible, get Ms. Troutman and my finance man, Mark Fineman, and bring them in here. I'd like you to return and post two of your best men outside for extra protection."

"Yes, sir." Palmer threw a quick frown in Brandon's direction, then left the room.

Realizing Brandon was in the mood to cause trouble and Angie was about to be in his line of fire, Lowell issued a new warning. "I expect you to be quiet and respectful as soon as our guests arrive."

"I didn't hear my name on the list of approved people who get to stay."

"One more comment like that and you can fend for yourself outside like everyone else."

AARON STARED AT THE SMALL screen of his cell. If willing the phone back into service worked, the lights would flash. Something. "I can't get through. Since we've lost the comm network, we're on our own up here."

Royal blew out a long breath. "This is just getting better and better."

They'd moved farther into the open room, over by the windows and away from the body on the floor. Risa had seen enough violence for a lifetime. And he was ready to go a few minutes without someone tackling him or trying to kill him.

"We can try using mine." Risa patted her pockets. "Wait, I left my purse downstairs in the manager's office. Well, of course it is. Why should anything go right today?"

"It wouldn't work anyway," Royal said. "Someone is jamming the signal. Nothing would get through."

The "why" behind that action was the piece Aaron kept missing. The recent threats centered on Lowell. Angie had a bedroom connection to Lowell, but not a linear one. Grabbing a related woman when the true target stood just downstairs was the type of logic Aaron had trouble reasoning through.

But he had to figure out a workaround. He wasn't one to sit and wait, working on the defensive. An offensive strike was the answer. "Here's the bad news—"

Risa's eyes grew huge. "We haven't had the bad part yet?"

"Without the schematics, we depend on my memory of the layout of this place. I looked at a lot of paperwork and retained a great deal of it." At least he hoped that was true.

Royal glanced at the ceiling. "If you say so."

"I have to agree with Royal on this one." Risa leaned back with her head balancing against the window and let her eyes slip shut. "Except for the part where you know how to throw that weapon around—"

"Excuse me?"

"I wish you actually were a lawyer. They have to memorize a lot of stuff in school. That skill set could help us here."

Time for another shot of truth. Aaron wondered if

he'd spent the next month unraveling the lies he'd told her. "I am."

Her eyes popped open. "What?"

"A lawyer." He scowled at Royal, trying to get him to at least pretend he wasn't listening in. Some things should be private.

She looked at Aaron, at Royal and back again. "But that was a lie."

Aaron slid next to her with his hands balanced behind him on the edge of the windowsill. The space between them contracted and his fingers touched hers. "Just the tax part. Lawyer, navy JAG, to be exact, and now security expert. But, since I pay my bar dues, still a lawyer."

The words hung in the quiet until Royal snapped his fingers. "Uh, shouldn't you know that?" he asked Risa. "I thought you two were dating."

Her eyes sparkled when she answered, "Right now I feel lucky I even know his name. It is Aaron, right?"

The byplay had Royal grinning like an idiot. Aaron understood the goofy reaction. Something about the way she lost herself in a moment made that hard shell he'd fought so hard to build around him crumble. He'd seen it as she smiled over an email or described the perfect latte.

It was the reason he switched from talking with her over coffee to asking her out for dinner. Picking up random women over scones was not his usual style. He made an exception for her.

She leaned toward Royal and he met her halfway, as if sharing a big secret. "Your coworker—"

Aaron broke in. "Technically, I'm his boss."

"—has a problem with dating honesty."

"Now is not the time for this conversation." There was a dead guy on the floor and two injured down the hall. All of this amusing talk could wait. Aaron turned to Royal. "To be clear, there will never be a time for you to join in the conversation about my dating life."

Her fingers slid through his as her smile faded. "You're right. We're not going to talk about anything if we don't get off this floor alive."

He hated killing the lighter mood, but this was not the time to get lazy. Anyone could be waiting around the next corner. In fact, he would bet there was at least one more guy close by because he doubted these guys worked solo and they had an odd number down.

"Normally I would suggest we not exaggerate, but since three men have come after you in the span of a half hour, we need to assume you're a potential victim here," Aaron said.

"Gee, do you think?"

Royal held up a hand. "Except for the empty cartridges. That throws the whole scenario off."

"Not all of them are empty." Aaron hated to break the physical connection with Risa and regretted it the minute he lifted his hand. He slipped out one of the cartridges he'd emptied in the bathroom and chucked it to Royal. "These went with the first attacker's other gun, the one he pointed at us. They sure seem real."

Royal studied the bullet. "None of this makes sense."

"Shouldn't we warn Angie?" Risa bit her bottom lip. "I mean, these guys want her, not me. She could be in real danger."

He didn't want to scare her, not when they'd spent the past few minutes coming down from the adrenaline rush, but she had to be ready for the next guy who shoved a gun in her face, and Aaron feared there would be at least one more. "So long as they think you're the one they want, Angie should be safe."

"Then I guess I drew the short straw on this one."

Royal nodded. "Unfortunately, yes."

"We need to split up." Until Aaron knew what was happening throughout the building, just hopping on the elevator and taking a chance that no one would be there ready to fire was not an option. Not a feasible one anyway.

"For the record, I'm sticking with you." She eyed him as if daring them to disagree. "You ran into the bathroom and now you're stuck with me."

"Agreed. You're not leaving my side." How he'd gone from forgetting to call her to not wanting to leave her, he wasn't sure, but this went beyond offering protection.

Her shoulders relaxed. "What are we going to do?"

Aaron started with Royal. "Try the roof. See if you can get the phone or the comm to work. We'll check the floor to make sure it's clear."

She made a face. "Really? Because at this point I vote for hiding."

Though it was not his style and not his job, she needed reassurance and he'd give it to her. "It just might come to that."

Chapter Six

Angie paced around the small conference table. Five people in a twelve-by-twelve space and one of them a twenty-something with an attitude and a staring problem. Not her idea of fun.

Being locked in a room with Lowell was one thing. They'd spent hours in hotels and even a few nights in his big house behind the high fence while Sonya was away. Right in her king-size bed, on those thousand-dollar sheets Angie knew the other woman had scoured the stores picking out.

The memory of walking around naked in Lowell's country estate made her smile. Hunting through the other woman's closet, touching her clothes and trying on her jewelry had given her satisfaction. All those hours of exploring almost made putting up with Lowell's mood swings worthwhile.

It had been so tempting to take the rubies with her. Just slip them into her overnight bag and sneak them home. Heaven knew she'd earned them. Listening to Lowell. Being with Lowell. As far as Angie was concerned, her job was far harder and more taxing than that of wife.

If only sleeping with the boss carried the same financial benefit. But she intended to rectify the deficiency as soon as she figured out what was happening right now.

Mark Fineman stepped in front of her and handed her a glass of something she assumed was eggnog. "You seem pretty happy for someone being held in a room at a lame holiday party."

"I've had worse."

That went for the situation and the finance guy. He had just inched into his forties, but thanks to the marathon running he talked about incessantly and the countless hours in the gym, he possessed an enviable trim waist. And brown hair that appeared to be all his, and a handsome face that likely once hooked women in college bars across the country.

He had potential, but he also had an ex-wife, and if the rumor was correct, a hefty alimony payment. Apparently his wandering eye and skillful hands had cost him big the first time around. He'd lost the house, part of his income and now depended on his fancy new sports car to start a conversation with a lady.

"You okay?" he asked.

She doubted the concern was real. More likely he decided it was time to make a run at a woman with more power in the office than his usual targets. He'd already worked his way through two interns and an assistant. Angie admired his goal in aiming higher this time around, but he needed to point his radar in a different direction. One nowhere near her.

"Why wouldn't I be fine?" she asked him over the rim of her glass as she took a sip.

Mark glanced at Brandon. "This is a tense situation."

Angie wondered if Mark expected some expression of guilt or evidence of shame. If so, he was looking at the wrong woman. She'd built a life and did it using the assets her mother had passed to her. If that meant not being the office favorite, so be it. Those nitwit women bugged her anyway. They were just jealous she had the thought to start climbing the office ladder first.

If her life's choices meant upsetting an overgrown kid who didn't understand the realities of his parents' messed-up marriage, fine. She did what she had to do to survive and she refused to apologize for her drive. Brandon had everything handed to him. She didn't. As far as she was concerned, she was evening the odds.

"Are you standing here because you think I need protection from something?" she asked Mark. The idea was laughable, but she knew men often bought into those foolish thoughts.

"My guess is you have a guardian angel with more power than I have around here."

Mark grew less interesting by the minute. "I also have nothing to hide."

"Fair enough."

Lowell glared at her from across the room. Then his attention turned to Mark. With a flick of his wrist Lowell had his subordinate scurrying around the desk to his side. *Pitiful.*

No way was she running when Lowell snapped his fingers. She wasn't even supposed to be in this room. She should be on a higher floor, working through the steps she'd memorized. It all fell apart when Aaron McBain went hunting where he didn't belong.

When she regrouped and adjusted her plan, she'd be sure to take care of McBain first. She wouldn't give the man a second chance to ruin everything.

Risa vowed never to attend another holiday party. She might skip Christmas this year all together. She hadn't planned to go anywhere anyway. With her parents gone, what little family she had scattered all over the U.S. and out of contact, and her personal life in repair mode, she didn't have a lot of options.

When Paul had emptied their joint bank account and moved out, sticking her with a rent payment she couldn't afford, he'd made her life miserable. Then there were the credit cards he'd opened in her name and then didn't pay. He'd ruined her credit, which led to her losing her bank job and many friends. Amazing how they assumed she was the problem rather than the victim, which made her wonder about the stories Paul had told her friends while she was out of the room.

The engineers at Buchanan had given her a chance to start over. She appreciated it, coveted it, but she wasn't willing to die for it.

"You're doing great."

When she glanced up from staring at her hands, Aaron was looking at her. Those eyes gave away his concern. He acted tough and in charge, and he was, but she spied a layer of worry underneath. That bit of humanity made her heart turn over.

"I feel like I'm ten seconds away from imploding."

He brushed the back of his hand against her cheek. "That's normal for the situation."

She leaned into his hand and missed the touch the second after he pulled back. "I have no idea how you can use that word."

"Situation?"

"Normal."

A smile broke across his face. "Ah, that one."

"Why did you lie?" She hadn't meant to ask the question. Not now, not here. It popped out and she had no idea how to stuff it back in.

But since it was out there, all she wanted in the world, in that moment, other than to live from one minute to the next, was to understand his choices. When he went back to scanning the room in his stiff stance and with his flat mouth, she thought he was going to let the question hang there without an answer.

She sighed. "How long do we wait for Royal to come back?"

"You seemed content." Aaron had turned his back to her, acting like a human shield, and pitched his voice low.

She heard him. Understanding the words took more effort. "What does that mean?"

He shifted until his body lined up next to hers. He didn't face her. He stared ahead while his arm kissed her shoulder. "I live this bizarre life that sometimes comes with danger, and you sat in a coffeehouse humming some strange tune I'd never heard before and working on papers. I didn't even intend to approach you that first time."

"Why did you?"

He laughed. "I have no idea."

"So the tax thing isn't a line you use on all the ladies?"

He glanced at her then. One eyebrow lifted along with the corners of his mouth. "If I was making a play I would have said something sexier."

"Real estate attorney?"

"Pilot. Firefighter. You seemed too smart for this one, but astronaut."

"Oh, that's kind of sexy." Though she had to say, any guy with a gun and the whole ability-to-rescue thing was now number one on her hot-male-occupations list.

His body stiffened. It was as if every muscle clicked to alert status. "Problem."

The change in him had her snapping to attention. "Another one?"

"Do you know how to shoot?"

"A gun?"

"Forget the long lesson. Take this." He slipped a small gun out of an ankle holster and handed it to her.

The metal felt odd in her hands. She'd never handled a gun but expected something different. Something light and sleek that filled her with power.

She suspected the churning in her chest was more like dread. "I don't think I can kill anyone."

"Even if they're coming at you?"

Forget being girlie. She wanted to live. "I just squeeze the trigger, right?"

He pointed out the safety and angled her so her back was flush against the solid corner of the room with nothing behind her and an unobstructed view in front, "Don't shoot me or Royal, but don't give anyone else even a second to talk. No hesitation."

"You make it sound easy." She turned the gun over in her hands, knowing holding it and shooting it were two very different things.

He kissed her forehead. "I'll be right back."

"You heard something."

"Sensed something." He took a few steps, this time heading toward the left, down the part of the hallway they hadn't explored.

When Royal slipped around the corner and back into the open area in front of Aaron, both men froze in shooting position. All movement slowed, then cut off, as if someone had hit a giant stop button.

When their shoulders fell, her breathing started again. "False alarm."

"I almost shot you." Aaron lowered the gun to his side.

"Never would have gotten off the shot in time. I'm an expert at this sort of thing, remember?"

"What did you find on the roof?"

"Nothing. The door at the top of the stairwell has a lock on it."

She wasn't a security expert, but she knew about fire code. "That doesn't sound safe. Maybe it's part of the center's soft opening. One of the glitches."

Royal's lips twisted in a frown. "It looked out of place."

"I'm guessing we just figured out what these guns were doing up here." When she frowned, Aaron continued explaining. "Blocking possible exits."

Hope shriveled inside her. "There's no way to misinterpret that. They trapped us inside."

Something in her expression had Aaron turning back to Royal. "You sure there's no way through?"

"This isn't my first day on the job. I can shoot the lock off, but there's a soldering iron on the floor and a tight seal around the door. Unless you're carrying explosives, we're out of luck on this one."

While they argued gun size and trigger speed, she rested her cheek against the cool glass. She hadn't realized her skin was on fire until she felt the relief.

In the time they'd been stuck in there, the sun had gone down and the sky had turned a soft gray. Flurries blew around under the streetlights, giving the trees Christmas-card softness.

Movement caught her attention. She saw people in the parking lot and walking around the grounds. There was enough light to see Elan staff huddled in groups and several partygoers heading to cars but being rounded up by men in suits.

Since Craft was the only group in the building except for a few strays like her, there were limited explanations. "Aaron? Everyone is outside."

"What?" Both men rushed to her position at the window, but he got there first.

As far as she could see, the outside gathering was just one more incomprehensible event in a sequence of confusion. "Is the party over? And who are the guys in suits?"

Aaron put his hand against the glass. "They're mine and they're keeping people from leaving, which means they know something is wrong and they're protecting evidence and witnesses."

Royal lowered his weapon. "Good training will do that."

"I don't see Craft."

"Or Palmer," Royal said.

She'd never even heard the second name. At least, she couldn't remember hearing it. So much had happened in such a short time. She could no longer keep track of everything. "Who is that?"

"The head of Craft's security."

The new information had her head spinning. "I thought that was your job."

"I'm outside security. I own a company that provides backup in situations like these and takes the lead on others."

Just when she figured out a definition for him, he changed the rules again. "A lawyer and a businessman."

A small squeak of hinges had them all turning in the

general direction of the stairway to the right, the same one Risa had used to get to this floor.

Aaron put a finger against his lips as he pushed her behind him. When she looked up, she stared at two wide backs. In the span of two seconds, they had closed in around her in a protective wall of male.

"Stevens." The whisper of a male voice carried down the silent hall and bounced off the open beams of the construction zone. Footsteps echoed against the new floorboards. "What the hell?"

She guessed he'd found the barricaded bathroom door. This would be the start of the next wave of attacks. The danger kept ratcheting up and taking her heartbeat with it.

She'd give anything to be one of the lucky ones standing outside in the cold night air.

"We take this one alive." Aaron spoke so low she would have thought he mouthed the words except she heard them.

She wanted to grab on to both her protectors and run screaming in the opposite direction. More shooting. The chance for more violence. The thought of Aaron being hurt...or worse. It all sent her stomach flopping.

Aaron pointed to the closest corner. "Stand there. Do not come out unless I tell you."

She grabbed his sleeve before he could run away. "Aaron?"

"What is it?"

She wanted to say the words that would mean something in the moment. The right phrase to thank him for risking his life—again—but it didn't come to her. So she leaned in and kissed him quick on the cheek. She wanted to say or do more, but the timing was wrong.

"Please be careful."

He winked at her.

With soundless steps, Royal and Aaron crept across the room. They shifted in tandem, sweeping their guns and using hand signals to coordinate their movements. Not that they needed to go in covert. From the grunting and clanking, the newest attacker wasn't exactly trying to be quiet.

They slipped around the corner one at a time. She had no idea how they kept from making noise, how the guy at the bathroom didn't feel them coming. They weren't exactly small.

When they moved out of sight, her full-fledged panic returned. Knowing they were tough and in charge was one thing. Seeing them control the situation would be better.

Just when she was about to race across the room, she heard a loud click.

"Don't move!" Aaron's shout thundered through the building.

She couldn't stand there one more second. He'd yell, but she had to know what was happening.

Chapter Seven

"We need to get out of here."

Even at his son's outburst, Lowell didn't look away from the information Palmer had spread out across the table. He stared at the set of floor plans and list of potential attack and rescue scenarios as he and the others sat around in chairs in relative quiet.

All but his difficult son.

Brandon walked around the room until he stood at the opposite end of the table, huffing and sighing and generally making sure everyone was watching him. The boy just did not know when to stop.

When no one talked to him or asked for his opinion, Brandon started the whole procedure again. If this went on for a few hours, he'd wear a track in the carpet.

"Not now, Brandon."

The order didn't work. The kid slapped a hand against the table. "Listen, this is not that hard. We can walk out the front door and call the police."

Lowell was not impressed with the outburst. From the way Mark and Angie stared at Brandon, they weren't, either. "We are cut off from everything and everyone."

"We don't have to be. There's a roomful of people just down the hall. This is a hotel. People work here. I'm sure the town has a police force. We are the ones causing the separation, and that is more dangerous than being in a group."

"You're forgetting one very important piece of the puzzle. We also have missing security personnel. Until I know where they are and what, if anything, has happened to them, Palmer believes the company's integral personnel should remain in here, in a contained environment." Lowell leaned back in his chair.

If Brandon wanted a semipublic scene, Lowell had no trouble giving him one. He needed an outlet for the fury burning through his gut at having been targeted at his office Christmas party. He'd taken the precautions, hired the personnel and still someone got through. Someone who was wasting his time with nonsense.

"You see, Brandon, this is a grown-up situation. One where we have to weigh the pros and cons and not just rush in and do what feels right. There are consequences. That's the lesson I cannot seem to get through to you. It's not one of your video games."

"I haven't played those in years, not that you know anything about my life. Not that any of that is even relevant to the discussion."

"Everyone knows about your life. It's been in the news and the subject of gossip all over town."

Brandon's jaw clenched. "This is not about me. We are sitting here, waiting to get attacked, when we should be moving."

Lowell hated to admit it and would never say it out loud, but the kid had a point. Lowell questioned the current strategy. He also wondered if the man he hired for protection was really working against him. The idea of Aaron being taken out was hard to imagine. That left few options.

For more than a half hour, Lowell had been mentally

running through the people who benefitted from him being removed from the company. There were so few, but that's exactly what the threats demanded. Aaron's initial insight might have been correct—this wasn't about money. This felt personal, as if someone wanted him destroyed.

When the silence dragged on, Angie cleared her throat. "Your father knows what he's doing."

"No one is talking to you."

"Since I am part of this company and you're not, you should watch how you talk to me."

Brandon leaned across the table, his fury alive and flailing. "I do not have to listen to you."

"Your father is right about you. You're a spoiled brat."

"Shut up."

Angie looked at Lowell, but he wasn't inclined to step in just yet. Not when Brandon finally showed some toughness in front of others instead of cowering behind his family name.

Her chin rose in a sign of defiance he'd seen before. She aimed whatever anger streamed through her at Brandon. "How dare you talk to me that way?"

"You are nothing more than my father's—"

Lowell snapped out of his wait-and-see stance. "Brandon, that's enough."

"You're right." He pushed off the table and stood up. "I'm leaving. I'm not a kid anymore. I don't need to wait for permission."

Palmer stepped in front of the room's only door, blocking any exit. "No one is going anywhere until I figure out who started all of this."

"What are you saying?"

"Exactly what you think."

"You believe it was me." Brandon said it as a statement instead of a question.

"I think everyone is suspect at the moment." Palmer pointed at a chair. "So sit."

RISA DIDN'T WAIT FOR AN invitation. She jogged to the corner of the room where it emptied into the hallway and peeked around. In the precious few seconds it took for her to get across the room, Aaron and Royal had taken over and subdued the newest attacker. Royal stood holding his gun while Aaron had the man on the floor and a knee in his back.

"Here." Royal slipped a zip tie out of his back pocket.

Aaron looked impressed with the preparedness but didn't comment. He was too busy tying the guy's hands and dragging him to his feet. And he wasn't exactly gentle. The guy had his head knocked into the floor twice before he stood up.

While Royal reengineered the makeshift lock on the bathroom door, Aaron pulled the attacker toward the main room. Risa tried to duck into the shadows, but Aaron's gaze zeroed in on her before she could get back into position.

"Too late," he said.

"I heard it was under control," she replied. Not that there was any real reason to hide. There was nowhere to go in the open room, and she was not about to go off on her own.

Aaron brought the guy into the room and slammed him to his knees, earning a grunt from the attacker. "It's time to talk."

The guy looked around, his gaze freezing on the body a few feet away. "Who is that?"

"One of yours."

"Real bullets." Royal gave his report after checking the new attacker's weapons.

The anxiety twisting in Risa's gut eased when she saw the guy's face. She knew violence came in all sorts of packages, even when the guys were young and attractive like this one. He couldn't have been more than early twenties with huge eyes and a baby face. There was nothing hardening or scary about this one, except the weapon. He didn't seem to fit in with the others at all.

"What are you doing?" the guy asked when Aaron paced around him without saying a word.

"Figuring out the best place to shoot you that will cause pain but not kill you. Well, not right away."

Her gaze zoomed in on Aaron. From everything she knew about him, this was a con, but then it turned out she didn't know much about him, did she? Still, she knew in every part of her soul that he was rock solid.

"Maybe we should—" She was ready to fight for the kid's life, but Royal waved her off.

"I didn't do anything." The kid rocked back and forth as his voice tripped higher.

Aaron stopped pacing and stood right behind the guy. He pushed the gun into the back of his head. "You have two seconds to tell me who hired you."

The kids fumbled to get the words out. "I don't know."

Aaron pushed harder. "I'm getting tired of that answer."

The kid winced but stayed quiet.

Risa clenched her fists to keep from reaching out and breaking this up. Instinctively she knew this was the right way to get the information, but she hated the threats and posturing. Desperation clawed at her. She wanted this over. All of it and now.

"This is ridiculous and you are wasting time. Answer him," she blurted it out, earning a fresh scowl from Aaron.

When Royal motioned for her to join him, she complied. The new angle gave her a clearer view of the kid's face. Seeing him head-on ramped up the energy buzzing around inside her.

Aaron leaned in until his mouth hovered near the kid's ear and his foot clamped down on the kid's calf. "Listen to the lady. She is trying to help you live to see tomorrow."

The kid's mouth dropped open several times before any words came out. "I was hired by my uncle. He's up here somewhere."

Royal walked over to the dead attacker and shifted him so his face was visible. "Is this him?"

Risa turned away but not before seeing the skin around the kid's mouth turn green. He heaved and she didn't blame him.

When the coughing fit subsided, the kid started talking. The words came out in a long, breathless stream. "No, I don't know that guy. There were three teams of two. My uncle came up first. I was in the second wave, but when the first failed to check in, we came looking."

The uncle was the blond in the bathroom. She'd bet on it. They had the same eyes.

"What was your assignment?" Aaron asked.

"I don't—"

Aaron tramped down harder with his foot. "Kid, I am out of patience. You have five seconds and I start shooting."

The kid squirmed under the assault. His voice turned breathy as panic radiated off him. "I don't know."

"One."

Her insides kept jumping. She was desperate for the kid to answer before something terrible happened. Not that Aaron would hurt him just to hurt him, but she didn't think he'd bluff.

The kid shook his head hard enough to knock something loose. "You have to listen to me."

"Two."

"I'm not even supposed to be here." He focused on her as if silently begging her to step in and end the torment. "I was a late addition to the team."

"Please answer him." She whispered the plea as tension choked the room.

"Four."

The kid's eyes followed her until she stopped looking at him and focused on a spot on the floor instead. Her heart ripped in two. Part of her wanted to tackle Aaron and the other wanted to grab the gun and hurry this up.

The kid said, "Please, don't—"

"Five."

"Wait!"

She looked to see the kid flinching away from the gun. He swallowed hard enough for her to see his throat move.

Royal exhaled next to her. "Now, kid, or I'll take a turn on you."

"We were supposed to be on this floor at a certain time to grab this woman." He peeked up at Risa. "We weren't going to hurt you."

The words didn't amount to an apology or an explanation. They didn't make much sense, either. "You have the wrong woman," she said. "Not that having the right one would make this plan any better."

"That…" The kid looked around at all of them. "What?"

"Why do you think I'm the woman?"

The kid snorted as though they'd all missed an obvious point. "There was only supposed to be one person, this brunette woman, on the floor at the set time. We got the place and time. It seemed so simple."

"How about now?" Aaron asked, the disgust evident in his voice.

"You didn't have a photo?" Royal asked.

"No. One woman in a specific location. We pick her up, hold her and then let her go when the word comes. It's all part of some plan to get money."

Aaron lifted his foot off the kid's calf. "So then she was supposed to be a hostage for ransom? Gotta tell you, that's not sounding as no-big-deal as you're pretending this is."

"I just know she wasn't really supposed to be touched, but…" The kid looked at the ceiling and floor, everywhere but at a person. If he had some big secret, it was taking a long time spitting it out. "Something went wrong."

Her sympathy fizzled. Probably had something to do with being on the receiving end of an ongoing attack.

She shot him her best you're-an-idiot frown. "No kidding."

"No, you don't understand." The kid tried to move closer to Risa, but Aaron pulled him back. "This wasn't a real kidnapping."

"What was it?" Aaron asked.

"A joke, I guess. I don't really know. It's just that it was clear there was nothing illegal about what we were doing."

"A nonillegal kidnapping? I'm not sure what law books you guys are looking at, but that doesn't make much sense." Royal looked ready to explode. If he shifted one more time, his weapon might accidentally go off. "And why do you have guns and bullets?"

Fear cleared from the kid's eyes. "In case something went wrong."

Aaron finally looked at her. "I guess it's good to be prepared."

"I'm starting to hate the holidays," she mumbled under her breath.

"Tell us what's happening downstairs." Aaron walked around to face the kid.

Whatever he saw in Aaron's face had the kid answering without trying to stall. "Most of the people have been evacuated. There's a group in a small conference room near the party."

Royal threw up his hands. "And?"

The kid didn't handle Royal's anger any better than he did Aaron's. When either man spoke, the kid seemed to shrink. Much more and he'd be in a ball on the floor.

She was just about to step in when the kid answered again. "We're awaiting further instructions."

"From?" The chill in Aaron's voice washed over the room.

"I don't know."

Silence pounded in on her from every angle. No one said a word and neither man moved. The kid had turned a strange shade of yellow-green, as if he was on the verge of throwing up.

Finally Aaron broke the quiet. "You know what that means?"

Royal nodded. "Yes."

When they didn't say anything else, she gave up on being subtle. "Anyone want to fill me in?"

"Inside job." Aaron's words resonated, and then no one said anything at all. They were too busy wincing and covering their ears as the building's alarm system rang out.

Emergency blue lights flickered to life and flashed from the small boxes in the upper corners of the room. The alarm wound up and then blared in a high-pitched beeping sound before repeating the process again. A computer-generated voice told them to leave the building.

"What's happening now?" She shouted the question over the noise.

"It looks like someone has moved on to plan B."

Chapter Eight

Lowell watched Palmer rattle the door handles before turning back to the rest of the room. The small area had broken into chaos at the first flashing emergency light. For only six people, they made a lot of noise. Everyone but Palmer's security man shouted questions and insisted they get out.

"The building could be on fire," Mark pointed out as he argued that they should run.

Brandon stood up. "I told you we needed to leave. Staying here puts us in more danger."

"In light of what's going on now, I have to agree with Brandon on this," Angie said.

Palmer held up his hand. "Everyone calm down. There is no need for concern. We are safest in this room."

Brandon tried to push toward the door. "How can you say that? Something is happening out there. Anything from fire to an attack on my father and we're here, vulnerable and just waiting to be picked off."

"I need everyone to sit down. Chaos is our enemy here." Palmer grabbed Brandon's arm and shoved him in a chair. "Mr. Craft, can I talk with you a second?"

Lowell met Palmer at the door. In a room the size of a small bedroom, it wasn't easy to find privacy and no one was making it easy. They leaned in and fired questions. When Lowell didn't respond, they turned on each other, throwing out suggestions about what to do next while sirens roared around them.

He put a hand to his ear to block out the alarm and all the talking and concentrate on his trusted adviser. "What's happening?"

"I wish I knew."

"That answer doesn't fill me with confidence. Also makes me question your credibility since it smacks of the exact opposite feeling of what you've been selling to the room."

Lowell had known Palmer for years. They'd thrown in together soon after Craft took a lucrative business running secured storage space facilities and grew it into a multimillion-dollar enterprise. He moved it from servicing small-time residential customers to being the place commercial businesses looked to for long-term privacy and storage solutions. They were the leader in the field, and the cash kept rolling in.

But creating an empire also created enemies. Family members raged at his refusal to cut them in or be their bank. Former employees who believed loyalty was enough to secure their jobs learned that he demanded results when he fired them and sent them packing from the building minutes later.

He insisted on greatness and eliminated those who didn't give it to him. His system ensured that he surrounded himself with the best but had also led to many threats over the years. The latest, which demanded he step down, was less about evening a score than about pushing him out.

He was not going anywhere.

Along the way while transitioning from one type of

company to another, Palmer lost a wife who preferred shorter work hours to a bigger paycheck. After that, their son died and Palmer ended up alone. Through it all, he never lost his commitment to the job. So when Palmer's voice wavered with worry now, Lowell knew to listen.

Lowell went with his gut. "Call the police."

"We still can't phone out."

"Find a satellite phone if you have to."

The siren continued to wail in the background. Lowell strained to hear the low rumble of Angie and Mark's conversation over the buzzing and squealing, but he couldn't make out more than a few useless words. The alarm blocked out everything unless you were standing right on top of someone else.

And Angie and Mark did appear to be rather close all of a sudden. Lowell couldn't remember ever seeing them talk outside of an executive meeting before now. This was her new ploy. She'd flirted with a business associate from another office the week before. Suddenly she'd turned on the charm to some of the executive staff, or attempted to, when she'd always found them beneath her in the past. It was as if she was trying to ingratiate herself, but he had no idea why.

She'd used a few days together over Thanksgiving when his family was out of town to insist he buy her a condo. When he said no, she'd smashed the favorite decanter in his library and made a scene. Threatening to remove her from the property had calmed things down.

Now he wondered if it was time to move on. After all, women like Angie were not hard to find. Beautiful women gravitated to power. He possessed it, which meant he could possess them.

But dropping her would be difficult. She had skills

and she listened. She handled the unpleasant items at work and eased his stress during the day. She gave him something he needed, and she knew that.

Maybe he should just buy her the condo.

"Sir?"

Lowell dragged his attention back to Palmer, but the disgust over Angie's newest and not-so-veiled attempts at making him jealous still boiled his blood. "Well, we can't sit here and wait for someone to attack me."

Forget the woman. Forget the inconvenience. Lowell swore under his breath as the reality of the situation hit home. This attack wasn't a test run. Whatever was happening was for real.

"We can't go out there and invite someone to take a shot at you, either."

"This is exactly why I brought on McBain. He was supposed to prevent this sort of thing. The minute the party started, he disappeared. Have we heard anything?"

"No."

"He'd better be subduing this attack."

Palmer wiped a hand through his hair. "I think we need to explore the possibility McBain is the mastermind behind this. The pieces fit. The escalation started after he came on your property."

The idea had floated through Lowell's mind earlier and he'd immediately discounted it. He refused to believe his instincts had wandered that far off track. He'd trusted Aaron and didn't want to believe that his trust was misplaced or that he had invited his attacker in close.

Having Palmer voice the concerns made Lowell's defenses rise. "I believe there is another possibility, one we've been avoiding. That Aaron and his men were our first casualties today. What are you going to do to ensure that there aren't more?"

Palmer stood up straight again. "The situation is under control."

"How can you say that?"

Palmer glanced at his assistant and then back to Lowell. "We are in lockdown in here. Whatever is happening outside that door isn't coming in here."

"That has been the scenario for almost an hour and we are not one ounce safer, as far as I can tell."

The other security man, Max something, if Lowell remembered right, came over. When Palmer nodded, Max delivered his report. "This is different from a voluntary situation. I'm saying the doors are locked."

"What are you talking about?" Lowell asked.

"We are stuck in this interior room." Palmer slowly twisted the knob and nothing happened. He shook it harder and the door rattled but didn't move. "The door appears to be bolted from the outside. I can take it off at the hinges, or try, but I don't know what's on the other side."

"They trapped us in here, sir." Max delivered the information in a quick burst. Then he turned to Lowell. "If I may say so, sir, clearly someone who works for you and is integral to your operation, close enough to know your schedule, wants you out. That's the only explanation behind the threats."

"Not the only." Palmer glanced at Brandon, who was staring right back.

Lowell heard the edge to the man's voice. "Meaning?"

"There is someone in here who would benefit if his father was out of the picture."

Lowell shot Brandon a look. He sat slumped in his

chair, tapping his fingers against the table as Angie and Mark's conversation went on without him.

Aaron had ventured down this line of questioning, as well. Lowell discounted the argument as easily this time as he had the last. "He doesn't get controlling interesting in the business and what money he would get is tied up in a trust. There's no benefit here."

Max cleared his throat. "There are other reasons to kill a parent."

Brandon's lack of respect was not a secret. But that was different from being a killer. "And easier ways."

Then there was the problem of weakness. Brandon didn't have the guts to take charge of something like this. He'd barely gotten through college and couldn't hold down the one job he managed to obtain, he'd lost it within a month. The idea of him acting the role of mastermind for something like this was out of the question.

Not that his hatred wasn't strong enough. Even now Brandon sat there, the rage radiating off him and showing in every line of his taut muscles and locked jaw. Typical of his useless generation, he wanted everything handed to him. The sense of entitlement never wavered.

Lowell hoped that Brandon would one day turn all his misplaced anger into actual energy. "What does your gut tell you, Palmer?"

"Someone close to you wants you dead, and the person has chosen today to make that happen."

Lowell had already figured out that part. "Then you better do your job."

AARON LED THEM DOWN THE metal stairwell. Three sets of feet tapped against the steps as they moved. The close quarters emphasized the sounds of their breathing and the rustling of their clothing.

The kid was tied up and gagged on the floor above them. Aaron had wanted to knock him out, but Risa had insisted they leave him awake. She'd argued about how helpful he'd been and how he was in enough trouble with being hurt. He'd come to take her, and she'd begged for his safety.

Aaron chalked it up to a difference between men and women. Once he found out the kid wanted Risa, Aaron didn't care what happened to him so long as he never touched her.

But the mix of softness and toughness inside her intrigued him. She didn't slip into panic mode, though she had every reason and all right to do so. She stood up, carried on and functioned as a good ad hoc team member.

She also liked to argue a point to death. Much more of this argument and his head would explode. "Absolutely not."

"I can help. I can get places you guys can't because I'm smaller."

He refused to give into her on this. "No."

She held on to the back of his suit jacket as they shuffled down the steps. Aaron stood in front of her like a shield, prepared to throw his body on top of hers if needed. Royal stood at the back with his gun and gaze scanning for danger.

The theory was any attacker would have to get through both of them to get to her. If they managed that, she had a weapon and promised she'd use it right before she raced down the stairs and out of the building into the cold but safer night.

"What choice do we have?" She asked the same question for the fourth time.

He'd used the same reasoning to take the risk and

get off the upper floor. They were trapped up there. He needed to know what was happening with Lowell and get them all on the ground.

Then he would question every person inside and outside the building until someone broke.

"We can try anything else." Anything that didn't include her entering into more danger.

"There is another team roaming the halls. And that assumes the kid's information is right and there aren't more out there," Royal said.

Aaron thought about firing Royal on the spot. "Whose side are you on here?"

"Just pointing out the obvious."

Aaron fell back on the same argument. The same plan. "We cover the floors until we get to the conference room the kid mentioned. Risa hangs back and we blow in."

"We could be dead by then." Her fingers clenched his jacket as she said the words.

"Not to mention the problem with going in blind. There are other potential victims here and we could launch a firefight without figuring out who is behind this," Royal said.

They hit the floor above the party and the conference room and Aaron hesitated. "It looks like most of the people are out of the building."

"They could have been escorted out to highlight the true targets."

Before he could reassess or pick apart Royal's argument, Aaron slipped the door open and peeked out into the empty hall. No construction gear here. The floor was done and ready for use. Better news came from the quiet.

They walked out and onto the main floor. Neither of

his coconspirators said anything as he led them toward the maintenance room. Without making a sound, they slid inside. There were closets and cleaning supplies, an electric box, vents and plumbing pipes. This was a maintenance pathway to the heart of the building. The vent system led from floor to floor, then to the basement.

He knew from the plans that someone could travel across the top of the rooms and use the lighting squares to peek in the spaces below. He'd made the mistake of mentioning that upstairs and Risa had morphed into commando mode.

He'd put an end to that right now. "I'll go in, get above the conference room and see what's happening there. We'll figure out our next move once we have that intel."

Risa ran her hand over the vent and peeked into the grate they'd need to use to get in. "Unless you plan on cutting off both arms, neither one of you is going to fit in the heating vents."

"No way."

"Big shoulders. Will the metal even hold your weight? And even if everything else works and you actually manage to get in there, I doubt that you'll be able to maneuver enough to get back out. Someone will hear you in a second. I am your only choice."

"Still no."

"It's either this or take our chances on walking onto that floor blind."

Now she sounded like Royal. He worried enough about getting her out of there without having to come up with a plan to rescue her from inside the equivalent of a toothpaste tube when this went wrong.

And it would go wrong.

"What if they hear you or you fall?" he asked her. "So

many things can go wrong. The chances of you getting caught are too high."

"Be reasonable."

Royal exhaled loud enough to be heard above the alarm system. "That argument is never going to work. He is not willing to risk your life."

She frowned. "Why not?"

The throwaway question combined with her clueless expression snapped Aaron's control. "Don't be stupid."

"Excuse me?" she said in a tone that sounded more like a lecturing schoolteacher than a questioning victim.

Royal moved an inch, putting his body slightly between Risa and Aaron. "Uh, Aaron."

Aaron talked right over him, half around and partially through him. The point was to get Risa's attention. "You know why. We're dating."

A sharp silence followed his shout. Except for the ticking of air through the vent, nothing made a sound.

After a few heated seconds, Royal broke the quiet. "Let her try. She knows the risk, and this is the least risky of all options."

"I said no." But the arguments and her determination were wearing him down.

"It's possible the alarm will bring police and emergency personnel, but I'm not counting on it," Royal said. "We're not exactly on top of other buildings out here, and Elan is not up and running."

It would be nice if Royal were a bit less convincing, but Aaron was not that lucky. "We have to assume we're on our own."

"Exactly."

Aaron felt his command over the situation slip. "Whose side are you on?"

"The one that gets us out of here and identifies the

conspiracy before anyone else gets killed. I know there are empty cartridges and the kid says it's a prank, or whatever, but we have one dead and two more possible by now. We can't depend on the hope that this is nothing but some odd sort of drill."

"Which tells us it's time to act." He turned to Risa and knew she was their best course of action. "Fine."

A smile broke across her face. "Thank you."

"For what?" He grumbled because that's how he felt on the inside. All raw and dug out and anxious for what was to come.

"For letting me do this. I know you're against it and it's killing you to give in."

"I'm an idiot to listen to you on this."

She shrugged out of her pantsuit jacket, leaving only a whisper-thin silky white shirt, and slipped her heels off. "And thanks for not hurting the kid upstairs."

"I refrained because you wouldn't let me kill him." He slipped his fingers through the screen to the opening of the vents and twisted it until he heard a snap. With a tug, he pulled the screen off.

Looking at the space and peering deep into the darkness inside, he wondered how she would fit. She had a slim build, but the space was tight. He hated to admit it, but Risa was right. If he managed to get in there and shifted the wrong way, his shoulders would wedge and they'd need the Jaws of Life to get him out.

"You don't kill kids except in self-defense." She shook her head. "Boy, does that sound weird when I say it. I'm hoping I never need to use that sentence again. Or even think about what it means."

She insisted on seeing the kid upstairs as a victim. That touched off a fire in Aaron's brain that he didn't want to analyze. "He's older than you think he is."

"And younger than you want him to be."

Royal chuckled.

Aaron gave up. "You win this round."

"I plan to win the next one, too, so we may as well get started."

She put his hands on her hips and turned her back to him. He scooted up close, then stopped. The point was to lift her up, but he hesitated. Feeling her body under his fingers, having the heat of her skin burn through his dress shirt, smelling the coconut scent in her hair, all brought it home.

"Please be careful." He whispered the plea against her soft hair.

She glanced at him over her shoulder as if knowing how hard it was for him to ask anything of anyone. She squeezed his hand as her gaze searched his face. "You'll make sure I'm safe."

"Here." Royal slipped a rope around her waist and tied a knot.

"What is this for?"

"If we have to, we can pull on this rope to get you back fast. If that happens, don't fight it."

Aaron wanted to kick his own butt for not thinking of the precaution. She had him spinning in circles. He looked at her and his common sense fled. Putting her straight into danger was eating a hole in his stomach and slowly rotting his brain.

She stared at the thick piece of corded rope and weighed it in her fingers. "Pulling on that thing would hurt. Like, rip off my skin."

"Hey. It likely won't be necessary, so let's concentrate on the bigger issue." Aaron put a hand under her chin and lifted her face so he could see directly into those dark eyes. "You go quiet but fast."

"Got it." Her voice came back as a soft whisper.

"I won't let anything happen to you."

She smiled. "I know."

Before he could lose control or do something stupid like waste their first kiss on a quick moment, he picked her up and lifted her to the grate. She went up and in without any noise. Her bare feet disappeared a second later.

Royal waited until the opening was clear. "You've got it bad for her."

Aaron didn't dispute it because he knew Royal wasn't wrong.

"Your lack of denial says it all."

"Apparently."

Chapter Nine

Angie rubbed her forehead in an attempt to drown out the siren. Just when it cycled down and gifted them with a minute of silence, it wound up again. She hadn't counted on the never-ending noise. She hadn't counted on a lot of things.

The plan had been so simple. Force Lowell to make a move. See if he valued her life and how much he would pay for it. Push the controlled man and test his precious rules. If his resolve could be shaken, all while under his false umbrella of protection, it would prove she got to him.

McBain ruined it. This unplanned lockdown ruined it. The faulty cell phones ruined it. The list kept getting longer, just as her wariness intensified.

She hadn't planned for the other events unfolding around them. That could only mean one thing. Someone was taking over her blueprint and imposing one of their own. The new game proved much more dangerous than the game she had envisioned.

Maybe one of her men went rogue, but she couldn't see an end game there. She'd paid them. They owed her.

She regretted not stealing the rubies and getting out while she could. There were other men. Other sources of money. Next time she'd find one who wasn't married and didn't carry a chill with him wherever he went.

"It would appear someone wants me dead this evening." Lowell delivered his comment from right behind her. His breath blew across her neck.

Normally she'd find the heat of his mouth sexy, but something else was at play. Something dark and threatening. She didn't turn around because she didn't want to see his face. Not now.

"I'm sure it's nothing. Maybe McBain's twisted idea of a drill. I could see him using a party to prove how much we need him." But she knew there was more to this than a misguided security test.

"How can you be so sure?" Lowell leaned against the credenza so his long legs stretched out on either side of her. The intimate gesture trapped her in one more way.

"No one has actually attacked." She ignored the fissure of dread that threatened to crack her composure. "We have an alarm and a locked room. McBain easily could have done that for your safety."

"A second ago you thought he was the problem. Now you think he's saving me." She could hear the misplaced amusement in his voice. She turned to see what he could possibly find funny about this situation.

"I, uh, am giving you options. This could be some sort of protocol we don't know about."

"You don't believe this is fake. You know it's very real."

The words zinged across her senses, striking far closer to the truth than she could comfortably tolerate. "If you are truly in danger, why be so calm?"

"Nothing is going to happen to me."

She didn't understand the turn in the conversation but didn't let the confusion show. Lowell despised weakness. It was why he cast his wife aside and found his son so lacking.

Angie had remained in his life this long because she never cried or acted the role of the damsel in distress. She gave him strength and certainty and followed all of his rules without complaint. Even though keeping up with those rules was exhausting.

Now she summoned all her acting skills to give him what he paid for. "You're human, Lowell. If someone gets to you, you could die."

His gaze scanned the room, hesitating briefly on Brandon before returning to her. "That's not how this night will end."

"I don't understand."

"Oh, this nonsense will finally end. I've tolerated it long enough. Frankly, I only brought McBain in because Palmer was so against it. I thought he needed the shake-up."

Only Lowell would see a death threat as an annoying nit to be batted away. She thought he'd taken the second letter seriously, but now she wondered if he'd just been toying with them all.

"You never called the police." At the time she'd been grateful because she didn't want people poking around in her life. More than one former boss might be willing to say a little too much.

"Threats are not the kind of business publicity I want. They suggest I can't control my family or the people closest to me." His mouth danced over the words.

"You can't believe someone in this room is involved." It took all her strength to keep her voice steady.

"Before I go home tonight, I'll know who sent the threats and who set all of this up. I can promise you that." He used the same sexy voice from the bedroom to issue his warning.

Her chest caved in on her. She opened her mouth to try to draw in enough breath, but she couldn't grab the air she needed. "I wish I had your confidence."

"I've never found you to be lacking in that department."

Her breath came in pants now. "Who do you think is behind this?"

His feral smile was like that of a predator pouncing on its prey. "I'm working that out."

He knows.

Somehow he knew. She didn't understand who had tipped him off or why, but the evidence stared her in the face. "You keep talking in riddles."

Brandon stepped up to them, interrupting the conversation. Normally that sort of behavior would tick her off. This time she welcomed it.

He never looked at her. He was too busy growling and scowling at his father. "I volunteer to go out there."

Lowell all but rolled his eyes. "The door is locked from the outside."

"We have five men here. Surely we can break it down. We ram it. We use the table. There is plenty of muscle in here to get this done."

Angie felt a kick of reluctant admiration for the kid. He showed more gumption and courage than she'd ever seen before. More than Palmer and his armed sidekick.

But that didn't mean she wanted to watch him die. She wasn't controlling this game or the outcome. She had no idea where it was heading, but she sure couldn't have any piece of it tracing back to her. Who knew how loyal her paid muscle would be under police questioning?

"What if there's a gunman on the other side?" she asked, hoping to bring some common sense to the topic.

His gaze never left his father. "I'm willing to take that chance."

Palmer stepped up with his hands up for quiet. "Does anyone else hear a strange noise? It's like a scratching or something."

"From outside?" Brandon asked.

Palmer looked up. "From above."

RISA CRAWLED ON HER HANDS and knees through the blue-lit tunnels. She didn't have to go far because Aaron's strategy and planning started her off close to the conference room. She could hear the rumbling of conversation coming from somewhere beneath her whenever the alarm rested between cycles.

The bigger problem was crawling on her belly without letting her knees and elbows thump against the inside of the vent. Every wiggly step took longer than planned because of the need for silence, but up ahead she saw a shaft of brighter light.

Hiding behind the alarm's screaming siren, she double-timed her movements. The metal clunked when she lifted her knee. She froze, waiting for shouts or gunfire or something. Instead, she heard the same raised voices beneath her.

They were fighting about leaving the room and a locked door. Someone was holding them in and she couldn't get a sense of who.

She peeked through the crisscross of the ceiling vent. The light cover blurred the images below, but she saw six people, two holding weapons and one female. That had to be the infamous Angie and the only reason Risa was even in this mess.

If she could crawl across the light, she might be able to get to the space above the outside hall and see what was happening out there and blocking an easy exit.

She shifted her hips, and the metal beneath her knee thumped just as the siren came to a rest. The thud echoed all around her, drowning out the heartbeat pounding in her ear. Faces looked up, guns aimed in her direction.

"Who's there?" A male asked the question over and over, his voice growing more agitated each time. "Look up. You can see a shadow."

"Someone fire."

She scooted back, not caring about the noise she made now. She tugged on the rope to let Aaron know she needed help. The increase in shouting started a second later. Crawling backward, she moved too fast and accidentally wedged her butt into an angled piece, a corner turn she forgot about. Shifting her legs back, she scrambled to get out. Tried to turn around.

A bang shattered what was left of her calm. She wrapped her arms around her head and lay as flat as possible. The ping of metal on metal whipped around her. She wanted to move, but fear kept her locked in place.

Aaron had other ideas.

The pull of the rope against her stomach choked out a cough, and a second volley of shots boomed around her. She tried to get her balance back and center her weight over her legs, but they went flying out again when the rope yanked against her.

The rub burned through her shirt and straight to her skin. Her breath caught and her side lit on fire as her body slid with a squeak through the vent. Her fingers trailed along the metal, trying to catch an edge and slow the race down before her body got ripped in half.

The world kept rushing by her. When her mind caught up with her body, the haze cleared. The yelling in front of her had faded and she heard Aaron shouting her name. The panic in his voice soothed hers. She stopped trying to slow her movements and let her body be pulled across the metal panels.

Air breezed up her pants legs as her bare feet left the vent. Rough hands wrapped around her ankles and yanked her down. Her toes had barely hit the floor when hands started roaming all over her.

"We heard the gunfire. Were you hit?" Aaron's usually steady voice wavered, but his hands kept moving.

"Aaron, let her have a second before you crush the remaining breath out of her." She registered Royal's voice.

When Aaron fell to his knees and pressed his palms up her legs, she rested her hands on his shoulders. Without him being there, her knees would have buckled and her body crunched on the floor. Touching him, running her hands over him, brought her mind racing back to reality.

The trembling in her muscles stopped when her fingers slipped into his hair. Even his scent calmed her.

"I'm okay." She swayed as she said the words. The spike of adrenaline crashed, and exhaustion stole over her body. She wasn't sure she could lift her arms if she had to. If armed attackers made another run, she'd be a puddle on the floor.

Then he stood again, looming over her with a severe frown that before today might have sent her scurrying. "Looks like the bullets missed you. Any injuries? Even if you weren't shot, anything we need to check and take care of?"

"I don't think so. Honestly, I can't feel anything right now." She slipped her hand over his cheek, loving the brush of his stubble on her skin. The violent shaking in her fingers made her pull back sooner than she wanted.

He grabbed her wrist and placed a rough kiss on her palm. His lips shook as hard as her insides as his eyes met hers. "I'm sorry I agreed to let you do that. So sorry. That never should have happened."

"For a minute there, I second-guessed myself, too. I really thought one of the bullets would clip me. They bounced all around."

"Never again."

"Right. It was a one-time thing. It's over." She soothed him because his drawn face and pale lips made her think he needed the reassurance.

Royal cleared his throat. "I know the timing is bad, but can you sum up what you saw?"

She sensed Royal was stepping in and giving Aaron time to regain control. Since she needed a few minutes to regain her composure and talking gave her the chance to think about something other than the horror of the past few hours, she focused on giving an answer. "Six people trapped in a room."

"Where did the shooting come from?"

"Inside the room. Definitely. No one else was up there with me and all shots originated from the same general point." She rubbed her stomach and hissed when the fabric touched her raw skin.

"Didn't expect that answer. Sounds like one shooter and not a group of rogue attackers like we've been picking off." Royal turned to Aaron. "Palmer, maybe?"

Aaron ignored the question and frowned at her as his gaze traveled to her hand. "What's wrong?"

"Nothing."

"I won't let it drop, so you may as well tell me now." His gaze kept returning to her stomach. Another few minutes and he might rip her shirt off, and not in a good way.

She waved off the concern even as she secretly hoped for burn cream. "Nothing serious. A case of rope burn."

He dropped his jacket behind him and rolled up his sleeves. "Let me see."

The man had lost his mind. She gave him a bug-eyed stare. "Are you kidding?"

"No."

"Royal is—"

Aaron reached for her. "Married."

Royal smiled. "But not dead."

She had trouble digesting the information. Her gaze flashed to his bare ring finger. "You're married?"

He held up his hand. "Don't wear one for safety reasons. They tend to get caught in things, which makes accurate shooting tougher."

She thought about slapping Aaron's hands away. It wasn't as if he'd so much as seen her bra strap before now. Stripping down was out of the question. Then there was the problem of the looming danger that never seemed to be far away.

"Unbutton your shirt and slip it off." Aaron tugged on the bottom of her shirt, loosening it from her pants.

The friction inflamed her already-bruised skin. She tried to catch the sharp intake of breath before he noticed.

Too late.

"That's what I thought. Nothing casual about this. It could get infected without treatment, and clothes are going to be unbearable for a while." He went back to work but slowed down, gentled his movements. He opened the bottom few buttons and with a soft touch and careful hands pulled the edges of the shirt away from her body.

Royal's mouth dropped open.

Aaron was more vocal. "Damn."

If their reaction was any indication, she was afraid to look down. "How bad is it?"

"How much does it hurt?" Royal asked.

Aaron's finger traced the skin above and below the injury. Even that kiss of skin against skin had her squirming. "A lot."

"We have to get you to a doctor. At the very least, you need first aid. We don't even have a kit. It's downstairs."

His pained expression—eyes filled with sadness and cheeks flushed red with an anger she believed spoke of a need for vengeance—was for her. She loved that he cared. She couldn't believe they'd gone from a missed chance of a date to a moment where the rest of the world fell away when she touched his face.

She also knew whatever they had and whatever first aid she needed had to wait. "After we get in that room, rescue all those people and make sure no one else dies, then we can find a Band-Aid."

The tension around Aaron's eyes eased. "All in a day's work."

Chapter Ten

When the riot of noise ended, the occupants of the small conference room slowly came out from their hiding places under the table and behind chairs. One at a time, they stood up and returned to their positions around the table.

A squeak of a shoe against the floor sent them all diving for a second round. That time lacked the gunfire and shadows on the ceiling.

By the time they'd filed back into place, tiles hung loose from the ceiling next to exposed wires. Broken glass crunched under their feet as the room croaked and groaned from the aftermath of the shoot-out.

Angie cleared her throat three times before she could force the words out. "What was that? An attack? If so, why were we the only ones shooting?"

"Who was that?" Mark asked before he dropped into the nearest chair.

"Now do you believe me when I say we have to get out of here?" Brandon headed for the door, only to be stopped be a shake of Max's head. "Enough waiting. The next wave could be a real attack and not just someone doing recon. If we ram the door—"

Palmer took up the position at the head of the table. "We don't know who or what is out there."

Angie watched the *Lord of the Flies* type of breakdown of leadership in the room. Arguments that worked just minutes ago weren't succeeding at convincing anyone, including her. Between the screaming fear bouncing around inside her and the very real pressure that came from having opened the door to this mess, she could not take any more.

She'd made a mistake. A terrible mistake. She'd refocus and move on, but she had to get out of there first, and she didn't see where she was one inch closer to making that happen.

She bit down on her lip as her gaze moved around the room. So much despair and worry. She saw it in the harsh lines on their faces and caved-in looks of their eyes.

Until Lowell moved into her line of sight. There was not a hair out of place on him. He'd taken a seat at the middle of the table, not his usual position. He watched the room erupt in chaos around him, wearing a smirk of satisfaction.

For the span of a blink she wondered if he was the mastermind behind today's activities. The cool demeanor and lack of panic made him stand out. He'd say those were the characteristics that made him successful. The ones that let him rise above the petty concerns that stopped lesser men.

She'd heard the speech a million times. She'd never believed it…until now. He possessed that certain something that let the world collapse while he stood on the sidelines working on how to profit from the destruction.

"It's time." His voice boomed through the room with the force of a megaphone.

"Exactly." Relief washed over Brandon's features. "Let's get out of here and take our chances in the hall.

If we stay in a group, it's harder for anyone to cause trouble."

Lowell folded his hands in front of him on the table as if he were holding his weekly executive meeting. Forget that he had just survived a gunfire battle. "I meant, it's time for the person who has been hosting this little party to step forward. We aren't leaving until we figure out who's behind this."

Her mouth went dry. "What?"

"What are you saying?" Mark asked.

"Someone in this room started us on this course." Lowell looked around the room, his gaze stopping on each one of them as he spoke. "It's time to admit the plan so we can all go home."

Mark frowned. "You can't be serious."

"Oh, I assure you I am." He leaned back in his chair and brushed the tile dust off his dark pants. "I've reasoned this through. It is the only explanation."

Palmer leaned forward, his gun nowhere in sight. "And what have you decided?"

"Brandon crowded me in this room. Palmer kept us here." Lowell pointed to one, then the other.

Palmer didn't take being implicated very well. His usual stern frown slipped to a look of disbelief. "Me?"

"Mark has not shown one second of worry." Lowell spun his chair until he faced her head-on. "And Angie. Seems to me you have the most to gain here."

Her mind scrambled as she searched for a way out of this situation. "I have no idea what you're talking about."

"My patience has expired." He glanced at the ripped ceiling. "Whoever it is, admit your role and I will only fire you. Make me wait through another five minutes of this and I will vow to do much worse."

Mark scoffed. "It wasn't me."

Brandon held out his arms. "It wasn't any of us. He's doing some sort of power play."

"Mr. Craft, if you'll pardon the brief show of insubordination, this isn't the time for this sort of shakedown." Palmer's voice grew calmer the longer he spoke. "There is real danger out there."

"From the gunfire, I'd say there's real danger in here, too," Lowell replied.

He glanced at his watch. "Four minutes."

ROYAL KEPT WATCH AT THE door while Aaron shucked his shirt. He'd have to jury-rig a bandage for Risa's wound. Besides, the plan gave his hands something to do other than pull her into his arms. Hearing those shots and not being with her had taken at least a decade off his life. His head still pounded at the thought of her in so much danger.

Then he glanced at the red skin around her waist and his mind went wild. His fiancée had walked out two years ago over the dangers in his job. She'd said she couldn't sit at home and wait for a call telling her something had happened to him. She wanted him to get a nine-to-five job at a desk and with a retirement plan.

Something safe and boring. No more guns and certainly not car chases and investigations.

She'd wanted to take everything he was and change it. When he refused to give in to her demands, she'd walked out. He could still see the empty apartment, feel the rumbling hole inside him, when he'd opened the door that night. The note that said she'd rather walk away than bury him.

He'd learned about distance that day. And he'd vowed never again to be in the position of choosing the life he loved or the woman in his bed.

Which was why he never should have sat down across from Risa in that coffee shop. She was a woman you came home to every night. She wouldn't put up with stakeouts or gunshot wounds. Her life was calm and normal, except for the hours she spent with him.

Lost in thought, he lifted his T-shirt over his head.

Her voice broke through his mental wandering. "What are you doing?"

"I want to wrap my T-shirt around you for extra support. You're thin, which is already to your disadvantage in this circumstance. You need the padding to keep from irritating the injury further."

Her already big eyes rounded until they took over her entire face. She gave him an unblinking stare, but every now and then her gaze would slip to his bare stomach. Not that he was complaining.

He folded the shirt and brought it around her middle, careful not to pull too tight. As bandages went, this one was weak, but it would give her a bit of extra padding. One good hit and she'd see stars.

He picked up her shoes and handed them to her. "We're heading downstairs. My men are outside and we're going to get you to them and then storm the conference room."

The rapid eyeblink signaled her return from wherever her thoughts had taken her. "It's too dangerous."

He slipped the shirt and jacket back on. "We're out of options. At least I know, thanks to the intel you gathered, that it's a confined space with limited bodies."

"But what about the people outside?"

Royal poked his head back in the room. "Our men are watching them. They'll be questioned and let go."

She looked cornered. "I still—"

"It's all clear." Royal motioned for her to follow.

With a hand on her elbow, Aaron guided her to the door. He leaned down and whispered in her ear, "We're headed for the bottom floor. If we get there, you go straight outside. Do not look back."

"That makes it sound like you don't intend to come with me."

He didn't bother to respond to that because she wouldn't like the answer. Instead, he focused on the hall. They walked with her sandwiched between them, their steps in tandem and their bodies close. No one was getting close to her again.

They stopped in front of the elevator.

She stared up at the lights above the doors. "Is this going to work?"

Royal continued his surveillance of the hallway. The sweep of his gun and gaze never stopped. "With new construction, the elevators work with the emergency system. You stay out in case of fire. That's the only problem we haven't had yet."

She made a face. "Did you have to mention it?"

Aaron jumped in. Time to put the new plan into action. "You take the stairs."

Royal nodded. "Right. See you down there."

Risa caught Royal's arm when he pivoted toward the emergency stairwell door. "You're not coming with us?"

"He's the backup." Aaron nodded for him to go before she could dissect each step and get them arguing rather than moving.

Aaron saw the floor numbers above the door change. He pulled Risa to the side and tucked her behind him. Ready to shoot, he pressed his side against the wall and out of the direct line of fire should anyone come out shooting.

The bell dinged and the doors opened. Risa jumped,

but Aaron didn't move. He listened for any sound or sign of movement. When the doors started to shut again, he slid his foot in the opening. With his hand in hers, he pulled her into the car and let the doors slide shut this time.

He stabbed the lobby button before putting his body in front of hers again.

She shoved against his shoulder until he faced her. "What about the conference room and the people in there?"

So much for trying to sneak something past her.

He found smart woman so sexy, but this was the downside. "We're going to the lobby. I hand you to my men and we go back upstairs to see what's happening there. I have some concern the room is wired with explosives, but someone on my crew can help with that. Someone else can take you to safety and bring the police back with them."

Her face fell. "You're leaving me."

"Only for as long as it takes to end this thing." He glanced at the numbers and figured he only had seconds before he had to be ready for whatever came through that door. "I want you to know one thing."

"What?"

He didn't touch her because he couldn't. One brush against her and his control would break, and right now he needed his mind in the game and his hands off her.

But later everything would be different. "When this is over I'm going to kiss you."

"Okay."

"Not just okay. It will be one of those long sexy ones, all heat and passion."

She smiled as she shifted her weight around. The

moves looked like dancing but likely had more to do with nerves. "I'm not arguing."

"But you're not understanding me." When her eyebrows lifted and her legs stopped moving, he knew he had her attention and kept talking. "This is going to be a hell of a kiss. The kind that knocks your shoes off and has you wondering why you ever bothered to kiss a man before me."

She leaned in so close that all he had to do was meet her halfway. He pulled out of kissing range.

Her head dropped to the side, sending her hair falling over her shoulder. "You're awfully sure of yourself."

"It comes from the slow buildup from simple dates to a complex disaster. This has been brewing. It's all wrapped up with adrenaline and excitement and now it's spinning out of our control."

She balanced her hand against his chest. "Aren't you worried?"

"About what?"

"Losing the excitement of it all." She closed her eyes for a second and pressed in closer until her breath blew across his lips. When she opened them again they were cloudy with an emotion he hoped telegraphed desire. "It's the perfect moment when all you have is the intake of air and a wealth of anticipation."

"Yes." His mouth slanted to line up with hers.

"When you lose it, it's gone forever. You can't get that prekiss part back, and that's a shame because it's the best part. Sometimes I think it's better than the actual kiss."

"If you truly believe that, I'm not sure you've been kissing right."

"But you'll teach me."

The whisper of words shot straight to his lower body. She was so sexy, so right and yet so wrong for him.

"Yes."

When the lights blinked out, he almost didn't notice because his eyes had shut as his mouth lowered. But he didn't mistake the sharp slam of the elevator or the grind as all electricity inside shut off for a second.

His center of gravity shifted as his body went airborne. With his arms wrapped around her, he twisted and flew. The hard knock threw them sideways into the wall. His back took the brunt of the slam, but he didn't miss her groan as he crushed her close.

Remembering her injuries, he put out a hand to keep them from bouncing and hitting a second time. He didn't know how much she could take.

By the time the lights snapped back on, they were pressed against the wall, but the car had stopped moving. Risa's face turned into him and burrowed into his chest. The crack against the wall had his vision blurring. He blinked several times to bring the small space back into focus.

She lifted her head and sent him a frown. "I hate this conference center."

"Agreed."

She let out an exaggerated breath, blowing her hair out of her eyes. "What happens now?"

Aaron glanced at the trapdoor at the top of the elevator and waited for it to burst open. "Nothing good."

Chapter Eleven

Aaron had barely said the words when the ceiling tile popped open. In that same instant he pulled his weapon. Risa didn't have time to even breathe before a man dropped down in the middle of the elevator car. He never lost his balance as his feet hit the floor. His gun stayed steady, too.

Identification proved easy. He was dressed like his friends, head to toe in black, and wearing a grim face that promised pain. It was as if the bad guys had an endless supply of these thugs. Except for the kid upstairs, they all looked as if someone had bought them out of some sort of mercenary, gun-for-hire magazine.

Refusing to get caught off guard again or put Aaron in the position of having to fight for her life, she pressed her body back against the corner of the elevator. No one was going to grab her from behind and use her as a bargaining chip. Not this time.

She ran her fingers over the buttons and jabbed the Door Open one, then winced when she heard the click.

The attacker shook his head. "Don't bother. I control the elevator."

Of course he did, she thought. It was that kind of night.

With their guns aimed at each other, the two men

faced off. As Risa watched, the attacker's barrel slid until it drew a line straight to Aaron's heart. Depending on how fast he shot, Aaron could hit the floor without ever firing.

The thought turned her blood ice cold.

Her fingers wrapped around the small weapon he'd given her. She'd shoot if she had to. Those were words she never thought she'd vow, but a woman could be driven to act. She'd reached that turning point.

"Let me guess." Aaron almost sounded bored with the newest assault. "You came for the woman."

"I came to stop you."

"Sounds like the plan changed. I'll consider that progress."

Aaron's jacket covered his back, but Risa knew he had a second weapon there. Between them, they were well armed and had to outgun this guy. Still, the attacker looked confident.

And that scared the crap out of Risa. Except for the kid who got separated upstairs, these guys came in pairs and attacked in waves. Seeing one of them in the middle of the room didn't mean there wasn't a second one roaming around. Where one existed, another hovered in the background, though she hoped this one was the second to the kid upstairs. Her only comfort was that if she'd figured it out, so had Aaron. He'd be looking, anticipating a potential secondary attacker.

But there was a limit to his line of attack. The space couldn't be more than five by five.

She glanced up, calculating the chance someone could stay hidden on top of the car but still shoot through the ceiling. If that happened, Aaron would be the likely target. He was the dangerous one. Risa wondered if she was now the add-on. That couldn't be a safe position to be in.

"What's the plan here? We shoot each other at close range and just hope the angle lets us crawl out of here before we bleed to death?"

She hated the sound of Aaron's plan. "You could let us go," she said.

The attacker made that annoying tsk-tsk sound. "That is no longer an option."

"Because we messed up your plan A," Aaron said.

"I don't know what that means. I just know my pay went up when I agreed to take care of you."

Sounded as if Aaron and Royal were right. This was an inside job and the person running it was here, watching and adjusting as things fell apart. Knowing they could see all the angles and didn't think twice about adding her to the attack list made her shiver. Her, a complete innocent stuck in the wrong place at exactly the wrong time.

The cold raced up her spine and exploded at the base of her neck. She wondered if she'd ever feel warm again.

"Put the gun down or I shoot the girl."

"No." Aaron didn't bother with negotiating or issuing a warning. He let that one word sit out there.

She almost wished he'd expanded a bit. To increase her odds, she pressed back harder into the elevator corner. Buttons bit into her back, and the raw skin of her wound burned, but she ignored it all to stare at the men in front of her.

"You're saying you don't care what happens to her."

"I'm saying if one more person threatens her, or even looks at her funny, I'm taking him out. You might want to think about that before you pick your next move."

The attacker shook his head. "I think you should—"

Aaron kicked out. His heel caught the guy's chin and sent his head reeling back. Instead of falling, the guy bounced back. The gun didn't so much as bobble.

Aaron pounced. With a roar he barreled into the other man's midsection and knocked the guy back and into the wall. The hand with the gun whacked against the inside of the car. When the guy held on to his weapon, Aaron grabbed his wrist and crashed it against the wall repeatedly.

With his lower body pinning the guy to the wall, Aaron kept attacking. He kneed the man in the stomach and threw an elbow to his jaw.

Risa thought Aaron had the battle won without taking much of a beating on his end until the attacker shoved back. He groaned out a new threat as the punches flew. A fist connected with Aaron's stomach, doubling him over.

Then they both went down. Arms and legs flew through the air as each struggled for the upper hand. Bones crunched and feet and hands pounded against the floor. A gun skidded out from the human pile.

She trapped the weapon under her foot and felt a surge of satisfaction. She tried to figure which man it belonged to, but she didn't know guns. Add to that the multiple opportunities each had to hide a gun, and the chances for bloodshed tripled.

With a hard flip, Aaron landed on his back, pinned to the floor by the attacker. She looked around for anything to slam into his head and came up empty. She wanted to hit him with the gun, but he kept moving and she feared missing.

The hidden gun in her possession, thanks to the guy's complete cluelessness in not checking her for weapons, gave her another chance at saving Aaron. So did

YOUR PARTICIPATION IS REQUESTED!

Dear Reader,

Since you are a lover of romantic suspense fiction – we would like to get to know you!

Inside you will find a short Reader's Survey. Sharing your answers with us will help our editorial staff understand who you are and what activities you enjoy.

To thank you for your participation, we would like to send you 2 books and 2 gifts – **ABSOLUTELY FREE!**

Enjoy your gifts with our appreciation,

Pam Powers

**SEE INSIDE
FOR READER'S
SURVEY**

For Your Romantic Suspense Reading Pleasure...

YOUR READER'S SURVEY
"THANK YOU" FREE GIFTS INCLUDE:
▶ 2 Harlequin Intrigue® books
▶ 2 lovely surprise gifts

PLEASE FILL IN THE CIRCLES COMPLETELY TO RESPOND

1) What type of fiction books do you enjoy reading? (Check all that apply)
   ○ Suspense/Thrillers   ○ Action/Adventure   ○ Modern-day Romances
   ○ Historical Romance   ○ Humour   ○ Paranormal Romance

2) What attracted you most to the last fiction book you purchased on impulse?
   ○ The Title   ○ The Cover   ○ The Author   ○ The Story

3) What is usually the greatest influencer when you <u>plan</u> to buy a book?
   ○ Advertising   ○ Referral   ○ Book Review

4) How often do you access the internet?
   ○ Daily   ○ Weekly   ○ Monthly   ○ Rarely or never.

5) How many NEW paperback fiction novels have you purchased in the past 3 months?
   ○ 0 - 2   ○ 3 - 6   ○ 7 or more

YES! I have completed the Reader's Survey. Please send me the 2 FREE books and 2 FREE gifts (gifts are worth about $10) for which I qualify. I understand that I am under no obligation to purchase any books, as explained on the back of this card.

❏ I prefer the regular-print edition   ❏ I prefer the larger-print edition
182/382 HDL FNNJ   199/399 HDL FNNJ

FIRST NAME   LAST NAME

ADDRESS

APT.#   CITY

STATE/PROV.   ZIP/POSTAL CODE

The Reader Service — Here's How It Works:

Accepting your 2 free books and 2 free gifts (gifts valued at approximately $10.00) places you under no obligation to buy anything. You may keep the books and gifts and return the shipping statement marked "cancel." If you do not cancel, about a month later we'll send you 6 additional books and bill you just $4.49 each for the regular-print edition or $5.24 each for the larger-print edition in the U.S. or $5.24 each for the regular-print edition or $5.99 each for the larger-print edition in Canada. That is a savings of at least 13% off the cover price. It's quite a bargain! Shipping and handling is just 50¢ per book in the U.S. and 75¢ per book in Canada.* You may cancel at any time, but if you choose to continue, every month we'll send you 6 more books, which you may either purchase at the discount price or return to us and cancel your subscription.

*Terms and prices subject to change without notice. Prices do not include applicable taxes. Sales tax applicable in N.Y. Canadian residents will be charged applicable taxes. Offer not valid in Quebec. Books received may be as shown. All orders subject to credit approval. Credit or debit balances in a customer's account(s) may be offset by any other outstanding balance owed by or to the customer. Please allow 4 to 6 weeks for delivery. Offer available while quantities last.

BUSINESS REPLY MAIL
FIRST-CLASS MAIL   PERMIT NO. 717   BUFFALO, NY

POSTAGE WILL BE PAID BY ADDRESSEE

THE READER SERVICE
PO BOX 1341
BUFFALO NY 14240-8571

NO POSTAGE
NECESSARY
IF MAILED
IN THE
UNITED STATES

the one crunching under her foot. She refused to play either card too early.

But she no longer had a choice. The attacker straddled Aaron's thighs as he landed a punch on his cheek. She winced at the contact and the dull thud it produced.

The gun appeared out of nowhere. One second the attacker was using his fists and the next he had a weapon aimed at Aaron's head. He bucked his hips and tried to shrug the guy off, but he didn't budge. After expending so much energy, he fell lax and his shoulders eased.

Blood trickled from the corner of his mouth as his head lolled against the floor. He hadn't passed out, but she feared that was the next terrible step in this battle.

If she didn't act, she would watch Aaron die in front of her. The mental image almost folded her in half, made her drop to the ground like some broken spring toy. The thought, so horrible, refused to leave her head. Trembling with a mix of rage and terror, she drew her weapon and stepped closer to the men on the floor.

With her hand shaking and her heart thundering through every pore, she stepped up prepared to fire into the back of the head of a perfect stranger. All thoughts of the sanctity of life fled. This was a kill-or-be-killed situation. Worse, it was an unwinnable game where her choices consisted of watching someone she cared about lose everything or sacrificing a bit of her soul.

She needed her head to stop spinning and the bile to leave her throat. The gun was in position with her finger on the trigger when Aaron went from what looked like a near unconscious state to a blur. He whipped a second gun out of his pocket and pressed it into the other man's chest. Without warning, he fired.

"Aaron!"

The shot vibrated through the small space as the large

man dropped on top of Aaron. He exhaled on a whoosh of unspent breath as the man sprawled over him. Aaron lay there for a second before shoving the guy to the side.

She was on her knees beside him a second later. "Are you okay?"

He struggled to sit up. His hand went to his side as the color left his face. "That's going to hurt in the morning."

Blood stained the floor and the crisp white of his shirt. Following his earlier example, she padded her hands over him. As far as she could tell, none of the blood came from him.

With a hand under his arm, she helped Aaron to his feet. They both groaned and more than one bone creaked. She wondered if the bruises would ever heal and how many showers she'd need to feel clean again.

He leaned down, swearing as he went, and grabbed two guns. With his foot, he rolled the attacker over. Blood flowed from his chest as his dead eyes stared up at them.

Feeling leeched from her body. Once minute she stood there aching and hoping for an end. The next, numbness raced through her. It was as if her body stopped functioning. But her mind wouldn't shut off.

Death hung all around them. She closed her eyes and saw the bodies pile up. When she opened them again, her mind played tricks on her, adding Aaron's broken and bloody body to the stack.

She swallowed back a scream. No sound came out, but Aaron appeared at her side. "What is it?"

"How do you live like this?"

His spine stiffened, making him grow a good two inches. "This isn't a normal day."

"I hope not."

But something set him off. Amazing a phrase made him tense like that but a fight to the almost death barely phased him. There was so much about him and his life she didn't understand.

His gaze traveled over her face, but he stayed quiet for a second. Just when the silence threatened to strangle her, he moved. He didn't bother pushing the call button on the elevator panel; he went right for the phone.

When he didn't answer any questions or say anything other than hello, she assumed the emergency system wasn't working. Not a surprise. Nothing functioned the way she expected it to.

Trapped again.

"Step back."

Before she could ask why, he slammed his elbow into the small panel above the phone. The first shot produced a crack, but everything stayed in place. The second hit knocked a chunk out of the wall.

Ripping off the cracked piece of metal exposed a mass of wires. "Know anything about electricity?"

"I was hoping you did."

"Let's try this." He yanked two wires. Bending the protective coating, he exposed the ends. "Ready?"

"No."

"Me, neither." He started to touch the ends together.

The casual playing-with-potential-fire thing had her eyes popping. She knew without looking in a mirror, her face registered shock. "Wait, are you sure?"

He touched the wires together and a crackle broke through the room. A second later the electricity whirred to life around them. Blue emergency lights popped on and a steady hum vibrated from above them.

She half waited for another man to drop on top of them. Aaron must have been wary, too, because he stayed away from the middle of the car and had her hug the door.

For the second time he punched the button for the lobby floor, and the car began to descend. "Let's see if we can get there this time."

"Royal must be going nuts."

"Unless he ran into trouble, I'm guessing he's jogging up and down the steps, trying to figure out how to get the car to move."

She could imagine him doing that. Aaron might be joking, but she could see either of them flying into a rage at the idea of the other being in danger. They were *those* guys. They rushed in when others dove under a table. Rescuers by nature and by heart.

"Very dependable of him."

Aaron double-checked his gun. "I know how to hire an assistant."

"After this assignment you should make him a partner."

"I like to be in charge." The car stopped as he finished the sentence. He shifted their bodies so his blocked hers.

She didn't bother to nudge him to the side or point out that she didn't want him to die for her. He acted on instinct and nothing she said would ever change that.

When the door opened, Royal stood there with his gun up and aimed. He didn't shoot, but she guessed another man would have. Something in his training had taught him to make that split-second decision, and she wondered how often he got it wrong, if at all.

"Whoa. It's us." Aaron issued the warning, but Royal's gun was already down.

"Glad you finally got here." Royal leaned over and

looked at the body behind them. His expression barely changed. "Rough ride?"

Aaron shrugged. "I've had worse."

She'd bet that was the truth. Bloodshed and a barroom brawl in a malfunctioning elevator seemed like a regular Thursday for Aaron.

Royal continued to look into the car. "Who's that?"

Aaron glanced down at the newest victim of today's strange activities. "I didn't ask, but I'm betting he has a friend around here somewhere. You see anyone?"

"Our guys are outside. Looks like they loaded everyone into an outbuilding. In bigger news, when the emergency system clicked on, the external doors locked. Probably some sort of end-of-world protection, but it means we're locked in this stupid resort and they're locked out."

"This conference center has everything." Risa let the sarcasm fly because she didn't have much else left in the way of conversation. The snotty comment matched her prickly mood.

"Except a viable way to get out." Aaron stared out the huge windows to the darkened shadows outside. "These are tinted, right?"

"We'll figure out a way to get their attention. Someone can go to get help, if they haven't already."

As far as she was concerned, her partners in crime-fighting were missing the bigger point. While she cared about the people outside and was sure they were pretty grumpy about being out in the cold, she was more concerned with the warm bodies inside.

Especially the ones with guns and a grudge. Now that they'd moved from what the kid had described as some sort of harmless kidnapping to hunt-them-down actual murder, her priorities had changed. "Any chance we're running out of bad guys here?"

Aaron blew out a long, hard breath. "I've found that rarely happens. The world seems to be filled with bad guys."

"That is not very comforting."

"But it is honest."

A fact Risa knew all too well. She'd lived that lesson and still did every time she tried to open a credit card and got denied. Even obtaining her new apartment lease had been an exhausting process. The credit catastrophe followed her everywhere.

And here she thought the worst was behind her. She'd never counted on falling into the middle of an active crime scene. This sort of thing happened on television, not to women who went about their lives trying never to bring the police to their doorstep.

She hadn't expected her day to end this way. She hadn't been prepared for Aaron, either.

"With my history with men, it's a nice change to hear a little brutal truth now and then. Of course, a flowery lie might not be that bad at the moment." She made the comment totally forgetting about his lies about his job and the false foundation beneath their relationship so far. They'd been through so much since then that it felt like a lifetime ago.

Aaron frowned at her. "Excuse me?"

The rush to apologize hit her, but she pushed it away. Sure, she'd forgiven him for the things he said and didn't say. She would try to work her way through that and understand, but it didn't change the fact that he'd lied and he should grovel for that.

Even without that piece, the comment meant something in terms of her past. She debated saying anything. If he had let the comment slide, she would have treated it as a throwaway and not important. But since he continued to stare, alternating between a scowl and a narrow-eyed frown, she searched for the right way to explain her pathetic past love life.

"Sorry to break this up, but we have company." Royal stepped between them and pointed in the distance. "The good kind."

Red-and-blue flashing lights lit up the distance. Police cars raced up the long drive to the conference center, their shrill sirens screaming in tandem with the alarm inside the building. She'd gotten so good at blocking the internal one that the police sirens sounded even louder.

Satisfaction showed on Aaron's face. "Looks like my guys did the right thing and called in reinforcements."

"Does that mean it's over?" She looked at Aaron as she asked the question.

His focus had switched to the chandelier above his head. The crystal pieces jangled as the fixture shook. Light danced as it hit the fine cuts. Her first thought was earthquake, but that didn't make sense. She still couldn't place what was happening when the rumbling started.

"Get down." Aaron shouted the warning as he dove on top of her. The blinding explosion came a second later.

Chapter Twelve

Aaron sensed the danger before he actually felt it. Having survived earthquakes, he knew the ground prepared to rattle.

When it bounced beneath his feet, Aaron dove for Risa. He caught her in the side, plowing her to the floor and twisting to take the brunt of the bone-shaking fall. His arms wrapped around her as he folded her underneath him and rolled. He kept going until his body hit a table in the open entry and knocked it over on top of them.

The air whooshed over their heads with a giant sucking sound. The thundering roar of a bang came next. Glass shattered all around them as the windows caved in and the walls shook.

With a crack, a piece of the far wall broke off. It smashed against the floor, breaking into tiny pieces.

Above them, the impressive lobby windows splintered and rained pieces down on them. They would have been sliced and mutilated if the safety glass hadn't exploded into tiny cubes. The tiny pelts clicked against the floor and covered his body.

Screaming and yelling sounded all around him. He couldn't process the noise or figure out where it was coming from or how so few people could be so loud.

Ironically, the wailing alarm had shut off, but the building was anything but silent. The crackle of a fire consumed the reception desk. A series of loud crashes echoed around the room as paintings and furniture fell.

A rumble from the floor above made it sound as if the walls were about to collapse around them. Loud bangs above them indicated debris falling on upper floors. He realized that the internal structure, like plumbing and electric, was being shredded and ripped apart from the force of the blow.

Somewhere off to the right, water ran. It skated across the floor, but the origin was hard to trace.

Aaron looked up to find them lying amidst piles of debris as papers and chunks of plaster blew around them. It had the feel of a postapocalyptic nightmare with everything covered in a cloud of white dust and a haze filtering the stale air.

It was no earthquake. A bomb had gone off. It destroyed the walls and everything else in its path at the once-pristine new conference center. So much for a soft opening.

When the ceiling above him creaked and groaned, he glanced up. A hole more than fifteen feet wide had been blown through the building. He mentally calculated the placement of the blast and came up with the party room. He heard jingling right before the half-burned Christmas tree fell through the hole and crashed on the marble floor a few feet away.

Just when the clanking stopped, a new round started. The bar above dropped bottles and glasses. One by one they shattered on the floor. Liquid splashed and more glass flew into the air.

The sound had him jumping and Risa moaning beneath him. He lifted his weight and turned her over with as little shaking and jerking as possible. If she'd been injured further, he didn't want to risk increasing the damage. But he didn't want her just lying there, either.

Her hands fell flat against the floor by her head. He checked her for blood and cuts and flinched when he saw both. He thought he'd covered her from the worst, but he couldn't be sure, and he worried that his body weight could have caused an unexpected injury.

He brushed his fingers over her lips. When her eyes didn't open, panic clawed at his throat. It felt like knives cutting into his raw skin. Everything burned and festered.

"Risa?" He choked out her name as he shook her shoulder.

Her head started to move and a small whimper left her throat. Aaron had never heard a better sound.

"Aaron?" Her husky voice turned scratchy right before she broke out in a coughing fit.

"Right here, baby. We're both fine. Can you get up? We're going to have to move." The walls continued to shed plaster, and debris littered the air and the floor. He had to get them out of there and to fresh air.

She shifted, balancing her upper body on her elbows. "Where's Royal?"

A new wave of guilt knocked into Aaron. He'd been so worried about her, he'd forgotten all about the guy who'd walked through these impossible situations with him. Royal was a family man and damn good at his job. Gail needed him for everything, and despite all the joking, he was a good friend. Aaron needed him to be okay.

He crawled over Risa, relieved to see her sit up on her own. He spied Royal trapped under a part of the wall and a broken table. Blood ran from his head and he wasn't moving.

Just as Aaron pushed whatever debris he could move off Royal without help, Risa appeared at his side. A layer of soot and dust covered her clear skin, and flecks of white clung to her hair. Ripped shirt, bloody shoulder. She'd been through one more attack and somehow survived. He worried Royal wasn't as lucky.

"He'll be okay." Risa repeated the refrain as she rocked back on her heels and cradled Royal's hand in hers.

Aaron felt for a pulse and nearly shouted in relief when he found one. Weak but there. No obvious broken bones, but the heavy debris lying on his stomach and across his thighs could mean internal bleeding and serious injuries. Royal was young and in perfect shape, but he was not invincible.

The main doors to the building broke open and a rush of frigid air rolled in. People followed right behind. Suddenly the empty room was filled with police and Aaron's team. Partygoers gawked from behind the line the police set up to keep crowds back.

The voices swelled to the decibel of a rock concert. Everyone wanted to know what had happened and where Lowell and his team were. People asked questions and a few of the more brilliant ones complained they couldn't take photos with their cell phones. Aaron was wondering about most of the same things, except the photo part, but he had a more pressing priority right now.

"We need an ambulance over here." No way was Aaron letting anyone get medical attention until Royal was loaded into an ambulance and on his way to help.

Risa would go next, and Aaron was not listening to one argument about that. She wasn't even supposed to be here. He'd introduced her to the place. He could help her make a graceful exit.

Aaron tried to stand and his left leg buckled. He slammed hard against the floor on his knees. The shock of the hit forced the air out of his lungs on a groan.

"Aaron!" Risa scrambled around Royal's unconscious body to get to Aaron. Using her weight as support, she put her body under his arm and propped him up.

"I'm okay." He was stunned and suddenly dizzy, but his injuries were nothing compared to what else they might find.

Besides, the show of weakness killed him. He understood the randomness of injuries, but he couldn't afford to get pulled out of there in an ambulance. He had too many questions and a need to be on the scene. At least for now.

He also didn't think it was serious. Possibly more of a temporary issue than a long-term one. He'd had a knee problem on and off for years. It would be just his luck for it to kick up and make itself known now.

Two policemen, clearly the guys in charge, pressed in on them. Aaron didn't need to show his credentials because he knew his guys had taken care of the introductions.

"What happened here?" the one officer asked as he helped Risa get Aaron off the floor. The other jumped as a chair from the second story fell through the hole and landed on the floor next to him.

This time Aaron's leg held when he put weight on it. "You've got at least six people trapped in a small conference room on the floor above and three more on the fifth floor. You'll also find casualties unrelated to this bombing, which we can walk through as soon as we get the victims out. You'll be seeing gunshot wounds on those."

He wanted to say more, but his gaze went to Royal.

Three guys had lifted the piece of the ceiling off his midsection. The emergency crew rolled in a gurney with oxygen and an IV at the ready.

Royal still hadn't moved.

Risa followed his gaze and her hand flew to her mouth. That's who she was. She'd known Royal for hours—tense and intimate hours but still only hours—and she'd already formed a bond with him. She talked about not trusting men, but Aaron found she trusted fast and deep.

A man could get used to that level of loyalty and commitment. Heaven knew he'd never experienced it before.

"He'll be fine." Aaron tightened his arm around her, finding comfort in the feel and closeness of her. "He has to be."

The EMTs shifted Royal onto the gurney and wheeled his still body out of the debris field and through the shattered doors and into the dark night. Firefighters rushed up the emergency stairwell with a medical team right behind them. The police fanned out as the Elan manager assessed the obvious damage in the lobby and peeked through the floor above.

When Aaron's head finally started to clear, his security expertise clicked back on. "We need to get everyone out of here. We could have a second bomb."

The officer directed personnel as he cleared out the space directly under the gaping hole. "You sure that's what this was? I mean, it sure looks like it, but according to the report from your men when they called us, it sounds like you've been having a tough time with recon for the last few hours."

"That's a bigger understatement than you can imagine, but yes. I can't see what else could cause this much damage." The only question for Aaron was the identity of the triggerman…or woman.

"And make that sound." Risa slipped her hand into his.

Her gentle touch in the midst of all this chaos and destruction fueled him. It felt right. He'd never been one to need comfort, but he now understood why Royal talked about finding it with Gail.

"My ears are still ringing." As a result, everything sounded muffled.

Risa shook her head. "I've never heard anything like that. It kept roaring. I thought something was coming for the building and would trample it. I guess a tornado or hurricane feels like that."

"Any idea who did this?" the officer asked.

Aaron had a short list. It included six names, some more obvious and logical than others. He had the puzzle pieces, but they didn't fit together in any meaningful way. This operation had the earmarks of skill and planning as well as signs of amateur fumbling.

The explosion didn't match with the fake kidnapping. There could be more than one thing going on, but it didn't matter how many there were. He would take it all apart and figure it out. The kid upstairs would turn. Someone in that room would talk. He'd untie this mess somehow.

"Someone in that room upstairs should know," he told the officer.

And very soon, so would Aaron.

ANGIE TRIED TO OPEN HER eyes, but she couldn't see anything. She blinked again and tied to lift herself off the floor. Something crunched underneath her, and her wrist thumped with a pain that ran from her arm straight to the headache pounding in her temples.

She had no idea what had happened. One second Lowell was counting and next the world crashed in on them. She searched her memory for an explanation, but none came to her. She hadn't passed out, at least she didn't think so. But the world was definitely not the same as it had been even five minutes ago.

After a few more tries and a bout of eye rubbing, she opened them. A gray haze had fallen over the room. The air looked like the sky the minute before a storm blew in. But they were inside, so the sudden darkness made no sense.

Using her uninjured hand, she pushed up to a sitting position. The world swayed and bobbed, but then it settled again.

Mark lay next to her with wide-open eyes. She started to talk to him until she realized his neck was cocked at an odd angle.

"He's dead." Palmer said the horrible words as he rose to his knees in front of her.

Palmer's jacket was ripped open to expose his bleeding shoulder. He had cuts all over him as he cradled his arm in front of him. Somehow he still held on to that gun.

"What happened?" She touched a hand to her head in an attempt to calm the thudding inside.

"If I had to guess, I'd say a bomb went off in the ballroom. It took out a lot of this floor and we were right in the blast zone."

His information didn't make any sense. She didn't plant a bomb or pay anyone else to do it. She didn't even know anything about the devices. For her it was too risky. So many things could go wrong in the timing and execution.

She had no idea why someone would use one now to get to Lowell. There were easier ways to kill a man, many of which didn't have the potential of bringing a building down on your head.

This had started out as a simple test. She'd gauge Lowell's loyalty and investment in her, maybe make some extra cash. How that had turned into this mess, she didn't know.

And if any of this traced back to her, she be on the hook for far more than a harmless scam between lovers. That was something she could make disappear with a little blackmail. Surely Lowell would sooner have her keep quiet about their bedroom secrets than turn her in. But this had blown into something bigger, something with the potential for actual damage. She wouldn't be able to con her way out of this.

"What about those people at the party?" She couldn't have those deaths on her watch.

"I hope they got out," Palmer replied.

"When and how? Was there some sort of mass exodus we don't know about?"

"The wall is gone. We can see more now than we've been able to for hours. Obviously, there's no concern about a lockdown now, but the need for vigilance remains. We still don't know who survived the explosion and what they want." Palmer pointed behind her.

For the first time she turned around and saw the extent of the destruction. She could see down the hall through the broken wall. Where there once was furniture and a closure, now there was a pile of something that looked like dust.

"Where's my father?" Brandon roamed around, stumbling as if he were drunk.

Angie saw the head wound and the blood running down his face and knew the kid was in trouble. Then the impact of his question sank in.

Palmer and Angie got to their feet and followed Brandon around what was left of the room. Palmer turned over a body, but it was Max. After a quick check, Palmer shook his head.

A movement in the far corner had them all racing to get there. After lifting some debris, they found a table balanced over Lowell's body. He lay there covered in ash.

He rocked his head from side to side, as if checking to see if he could still move.

"Dad?"

Lowell wiped his arm across his eyes, then shot them an unblinking stare. "Well?"

Palmer frowned. "Sir?"

"I'm still waiting for an answer." Lowell's gaze scanned his audience as he spoke.

Angie feared a concussion. He acted as if the bomb had never gone off and continued with the conversation he'd started before. "We need to get you a doctor."

"I'm fine." His voice sounded clear, but Angie wasn't convinced.

"Then what are you talking about?" Palmer asked.

"I want to know who's behind this." Lowell still hadn't moved anything but his head. "We're not leaving until I do."

Angie sat back on her haunches as a mix of confusion and relief washed over her. He was alive, but he was still a bastard.

Brandon paced and frowned, faltering more with each step. "He's lost his mind."

Lowell's sharp gaze swept over Brandon. The usual harsh frown he wore when he saw his son slipped and Lowell closed his eyes.

Palmer reached out to check Lowell's pulse. "Mr. Craft?"

When Lowell opened his eyes again, the arrogance that wrapped around him as easily as the expensive clothing he wore was firmly back in place. "I believe I had made it to number one in my countdown."

His comment quieted the room.

Then he passed out.

Chapter Thirteen

Risa never thought she'd be so excited to see the inside of a hospital. The smell of antiseptic and the beep of the machines. She almost cried in relief when an announcement blared over the loudspeaker.

Nurses rushed in and out. She'd had her vitals taken and her bandages changed. Each of them had offered her food, but her stomach churned at every suggestion.

She drew the covers up closer to her neck and shut her eyes. Snuggling down and settling in sounded good. Sleeping seemed like heaven.

She dragged in a gulp of semifresh breath for the first time in hours and inhaled the smell of freedom. When she opened her eyes again, she saw the fluorescent light above her and the ceiling tiles. A memory tickled at the back of her mind. Despite the safety now, something was very wrong.

She jackknifed to a sitting position. "Aaron?"

"Right here." His voice was groggy and more than a little grumpy.

She dropped back against the pile of pillows, letting the relief energize her. Exhaustion tugged at her, but she fought it back. Being with Aaron without bullets flying and walls falling was worth a few more minutes of straining to keep her eyes open. The need to see him overwhelmed her.

Her gaze shot to the side of the bed, and there he was. All disheveled with his hair messed up and the edges of his shirt burned. The tie was gone and the top buttons undone. His lean fingers hung over the side of the armrest, and his legs were stretched out in front of him.

He looked as if he hadn't slept in a month, yet he'd never looked tastier. Or less in control. His eyelids drooped as he sprawled in a chair pulled up tight against her bed.

Seeing him now compared to his usual state, no one would believe he'd held off bad guys and rescued her. The poor man didn't look as if he could lift a screwdriver without help.

"You're here."

A small smile tugged at the corner of his mouth as he reached out and slid his fingers through hers. "Where else would I be?"

Tears stung her eyes again. There was so much she wanted to say, so many things she'd figured out as her priorities had shifted in place on the floor of that lobby.

She settled for the other question on her mind, the one she dreaded asking. "How's Royal?"

"Luckiest man alive." Aaron blew out a rough breath. "Well, he probably won't think so tomorrow when he wakes up and can barely move but he's going to be fine."

She didn't know she'd been holding her breath until it rushed out of her. "That's great news. I didn't think… Well, he looked…"

"I know." Some of the sleepiness cleared from Aaron's eyes as he pushed his body up straighter, wincing with every small movement.

"Are you sure you're okay?"

"Banged up and bruised but fine."

She remembered his unexpected fall in the lobby. It would be weeks before she didn't see that every time she closed her eyes. "Your leg?"

"Messed-up knee, but I can walk. Royal is much worse. He's looking at broken ribs and a collapsed lung. All minor compared to some of the injuries he had in the army, but he'll be out for a few days."

Risa took in the information as she nibbled on her bottom lip. "Is his wife here?"

"Hovering and worrying." Aaron smiled as he said it. "She was concerned about you and me. She peeked her head in, but you were sleeping and she didn't want to bother you. I assured her we're fine and that you'd meet with her as soon as you could actually sit up without falling over."

The news had Risa's mind scrambling. "She doesn't even know me."

"That sort of thing doesn't stop her. That's who she is. She a nice lady who would do anything for you."

"So, like Royal."

"Except for being female and much prettier."

Aaron leaned forward and closed Risa's hand between both of his. "I'm just happy you're okay."

A lightness filled Risa when he opened up like this. He generally talked about work, what she now knew to be his fake job and general things. He didn't usually mention people. When it came to Royal and Gail, it was clear Aaron felt a connection.

For some reason that gave her hope; he could form that bond with other people, too. Like maybe with the woman he claimed to be dating.

"You like Royal's wife."

Aaron lifted her hand and kissed each knuckle. "I like you."

With that, her heart tumbled. Just took a spin and left her fighting to breathe.

Feeling suddenly self-conscious, she tried to run a hand through her hair but stopped when she snagged on something. No need to think about what was in there. She'd wash her hair fifteen times if she had to.

"I look like I've been hit by a train. A train that smacked into me, backed up and took a second run at me."

He pretended to assess the face in front of him, then shrugged. "Sort of."

"You could be more supportive."

"How about, you look like you got hit only once by that train?"

"Maybe you just like the smashed type."

The amusement dancing in his eyes cooled. "Is there anyone I should call? I called my dad—"

Shock filled her. "Dad?"

"How did you think I got here?"

She tried to beat back the blush warming her cheeks. "I just don't think of you with parents."

His eyes widened. "Wow."

"I know that sounds ridiculous." But something as normal as parents didn't fit with her superhuman image of him.

"My mom died a long time ago, but I definitely have a dad who insists on calls when there's a hospital stay involved. I figured you might have the same issue. That you might need to make some calls."

That was easy. "No."

"I know you're new to the job, but that doesn't mean you don't have work people, friends and family." He cleared his throat. "You mentioned something about a boyfriend. Should I get him here with you?"

"An ex." She brushed her fingers against his palm. "And I lost my parents long ago."

"I'm sorry."

There would be time for those discussion later, so she skipped to her point. "With starting over and being new to the job, right now you are my people. The two of us are dating, remember?"

He shot her the full-on sexy smile this time. "Yeah, but I wanted to make sure you did. Women can be fickle about these things. They wake from an explosion and want someone other than the guy they're with. Wasn't that a movie?"

Even with the cut at the corner of his mouth and the faint hint of a bruise around his eye, he was the most handsome man she'd ever seen. She didn't know if that was objectively true, but when a guy threw his body on top of yours to save your life…well, was there anything sexier than that?

"So, now what do we do?"

He pushed out of the chair and sat on the bed facing her. The mattress dipped under his weight, pulling her in closer to his body.

His hand caressed her jaw as his thumb traced her bottom lip. "I promised you a kiss."

That traitorous heart of hers went back into free fall. She felt every thump, heard every heartbeat in her ears. "You're not too tired?"

"For this?" His mouth hovered right above hers. "Never."

While his whisper still danced across her cheek, his head dipped and her lips pressed against hers. He skipped the tasting and the testing and went right for hot. His lips were warm, his tongue searching. The kiss exploded, sending a fire raging through her every cell.

She felt the kiss in her skin and to her toes. It heated her from the inside out and then sent a fine tremor through her. All control abandoned her as her head fell back into his waiting hand.

When she thought he'd break away, he pressed in.

When she wrapped her arms around his neck, he pulled her in closer.

They touched everywhere their bodies could press, and still their mouths kept searching. The kiss went on until her breathing came in pants and her brain signaled her common sense to pack for vacation. She'd just decided to drag him down to the mattress with her when a loudspeaker announcement broke the moment.

He pulled back and rested his forehead against hers. "Was that thing louder this time? I swear she was talking to us. Kind of felt like high school there for a second."

Her shoulders slumped in disappointment. "I'm kind of sick of alarms and sirens and anything that comes out of a speaker."

"Maybe true, but you haven't given me your assessment."

"Of what?"

"Do you still think the anticipation beats the actual kiss?"

Promise kept. "I was an idiot about that theory. Now I know better."

"Yeah, let's say you were uneducated." He pressed a light kiss on her mouth before sitting back and putting a foot of needed air between them. "But I gotta say that one took me by surprise, too. I expected something sexy, but I got a tiny bit of naughty in there, too."

"Is that bad?"

"Naughty is never bad."

Sweet-talker. "Imagine what we'll be able to do when we're not in a hospital."

She wanted to call back the words as soon as she'd said them. Yeah, he'd joked about another date, but this was the same guy who'd failed to call. A mercy date was bad enough. One grown out of the joint survival of violence didn't appeal to her at all.

She tried to laugh it off. "Forget I said that."

"No way that's going to happen. I have you down for more kiss testing. Count on me collecting."

Her gaze flew to his. She could play coy or wait for his next move. She would do all those things the magazine articles tell you to do to catch a man. Those same things she read and laughed about. Funny how they seemed ridiculous when you were in a relationship and maybe not so silly when you weren't.

But a strong woman said what she wanted. "Technically, you owe me a date."

"And an apology and several explanations. We'll talk about all of it. I am not foolish enough to think all is forgiven and forgotten."

"I'm getting there."

"Good to know." He picked a piece of paper out of her hair and let it fall to the floor. "But before I do anything else, I'm going to kiss you again."

When he lowered his head to hers, she didn't argue.

Chapter Fourteen

Lowell stood over Brandon's hospital bed. In sleep, the boy couldn't cause any trouble. He lay there so quiet and still.

Pressed against the white sheets with tubes sticking in him and machines beeping all around him brought back a memory. Brandon had had surgery as a kid. Both times his dark hair had spread out around him and a pain-relief drip hung nearby.

Lowell didn't do many parental things, believing that in the family division of labor those fell to Sonya. But medical crises had always been mandatory events for both parents. Right now Brandon's actions in messing up his job had Lowell furious, but he knew his place was here. Even if he didn't have this time to waste.

After endless rounds of pacing and numerous conversations that started with the doom and gloom of a lifetime coma, Lowell finally had to send Sonya down to the cafeteria for coffee to keep her from crying all over both of them. Only she could turn a simple hospital stay into a deathbed session.

A severe concussion, some broken bones and an unwillingness to wake up. The doctors assured Lowell the reaction was normal in light of Brandon's injuries. No reason to worry yet. With his age and health, there was little cause to worry that this was anything other than the usual protective coma the body did in these circumstances.

Not that Lowell was inclined to do so.

"He okay?" Palmer walked in with his arm in a cast and cuts all over his face.

"We're waiting for him to come out of it."

And Brandon would. They'd been lucky. Mark hadn't made it out. The police said something about other bodies, but Lowell hadn't gotten a list yet. He'd answered questions in the ambulance. The police had many of them, including why he didn't come to them with the threats.

As if they could help. Of course, McBain and his team hadn't been much better. Maybe Palmer was right about how hiring outside sources had been a mistake. Lowell had already decided to hold a meeting tomorrow to walk through what had happened tonight.

McBain had a lot to answer for, and he was not alone. Someone started this. Lowell would end it.

Palmer stood on the opposite side of Brandon's bed and stared down at him. "His first concern was for you."

Lowell looked up. "Meaning?"

"Injured and a mess, he called out for you. The room was partly on fire and crumbling around us, and he was the only one shouting for you. Not Ms. Troutman. Not even me. Brandon."

"Probably hoped he could find my wallet before anyone else did." When silence greeted his comment, Lowell glanced up. "What is it?"

Palmer opened his mouth as if to say something, then shook his head. "Nothing, sir."

"You may speak freely. This is your one opportunity, so use it wisely."

"I'm telling you he got to you first." The words

rushed out of Palmer. "I didn't hear any talk about money or the business. He wanted to find you and nearly killed himself doing it."

"You're dissatisfied with my parenting skills." That seemed fair since Lowell was not impressed with Palmer's protection skills. Something had gone haywire yesterday and cost lives, lives he'd likely be sued over, and Lowell was determined to hold someone responsible. If it was the man in front of him, the man he'd known the longest, so be it.

Palmer waved the conversation off. "I'm sorry. This isn't my business."

"You seem to think it is."

Palmer looked as if he was going to drop the topic, but then he picked it up again. "It's just that for a few minutes tonight I saw Brandon for what he's becoming. And he's not a kid anymore."

Lowell knew this was a touchy subject. Palmer's only child, a son, died in Iraq. He'd deployed and failed to make it through the first week. It gave Palmer a soft spot for Brandon, which infuriated Lowell. The last thing his son needed was one more person coddling him.

"Noted."

Palmer's face flushed, but he didn't pursue the conversation. "Yes, sir."

He turned to leave, but Lowell stopped him. "I want everyone in the office tomorrow—you, Aaron, Angie. It's time to end this thing."

"Sir?"

"Now you're dismissed."

"I LIKE YOUR PLACE." Risa delivered her assessment from just inside the door. She hadn't ventured out of the entry or even let go of the doorknob behind her back.

She stood next to the closet, looking every bit the lost pup in a new place. If she remained that still and lifeless for much longer, Aaron might have to take her back to the hospital.

He wondered if it was fear or just the result of so many tragedies. She's seen a lot of blood and death. The doctors had checked for shock, but he guessed it could be delayed.

Having her here should be enough. He'd been thinking of nothing else since he refused his own hospital bed and took up residence in the chair next to hers. But he wanted her healthy and secure, not terrified and ready to slip into hiding.

Looking at her now, he wondered if he should have insisted she stay another night. Once they'd both rested and made sure the sparks arcing between them amounted to more than a reaction to the violence they'd experienced.

The hospital staff had given her scrubs. The oversize and shapeless green shirt hung over her slim shoulders, making her look tiny and so very vulnerable. She had a smudge on her cheek and tiny pieces of debris in her hair. Like him, she desperately needed a shower and two days in bed to recover from all they'd seen and survived.

If he could have tolerated being away from her, he would have dropped her at her place and left her alone to recharge. But that plan made his stomach heave, so he never suggested the option. Neither did she, he noticed.

"It's a basic condo. Nothing special." He'd moved in after his fiancée decided he'd be better on his own than with her. Pam had picked out almost everything in the last place, so he got the leftovers and never bothered to fill in with anything else.

Glancing around now, he tried to see the bachelor

pad through her eyes. Beige carpet. Beige walls. Beige couch. He didn't have a lot of creativity when it came to decorating. He hadn't even put up a Christmas tree or anything else festive for the holidays because he didn't own anything.

There were better ways to spend his time. He was sure of that. He liked the furniture comfortable and the countertops unfussy, but he didn't have many other rules.

A balcony lined the far wall of the large living room. Off the main room stood the kitchen and the long hall to two matching master bedrooms. Tucked out of sight and off to the side sat the den, a room filled with papers and guided by very little organization.

He took a few steps and realized she wasn't behind him. A lame joke died on his kips. "Why are you making a face?"

She blinked a few times. "It's nothing."

"Definitely something." The stunned look suggested the "something" was pretty big.

He didn't intend to jump on top of her the second she got close, and he was ticked off she might think that. He wasn't an animal. He could wait for the timing to be right. Until then, he wanted to be near her, which was a new-to-him feeling he refused to analyze too closely.

Her eyes glanced around the condo again. "As someone who once lost a house, I can tell you there's nothing 'basic' about the place where you find comfort and release. Having a home is important. Losing it is devastating. It's not something I'd wish on anyone. Forget the embarrassment, there's the vulnerability of it all."

"Of course."

"Even if it's not a mansion, it means something. I'm

a nester by nature, so my home meant everything to me and I didn't realize until I lost it."

This wasn't the first hint she'd dropped about her past. There was something about boyfriends being liars. While that claim hit too close to their relationship, he sensed he was not the only man in her past guilty of that sin.

"Tell me what you mean by lost?" he asked even though part of him feared the answer.

Her gaze went to the floor. "Probably a conversation for another day."

Some things needed to be said. Besides that, he wanted to know all he could about her. All of her, the good and the bad. And if someone treated her like crap, he'd stand up and stop it.

"I'm awake now," he said as a way to urge her to talk. Though he could drop at any second.

"Once we're done with me, we'll start on you. So, is a walk through my past really what you want to do?"

"Not even close." His interest in the topic dropped to a crash. Dread took its place. When a woman wanted to exchange past relationship information, it never turned out well for the male of the partnership.

"Then why are we still talking?" She moved this time. She walked into the room and kept going until she stood right in front of him.

Her hands didn't move, but he felt her words with the impact of a touch. He gazed into her big eyes and sweet face. She looked so soft and sweet and the things he wanted to do to her were anything but.

Stepping back was the right answer.

He reached for her instead. His hands smoothed over her shoulders, letting the warmth of her skin spur him on. "I've made a lot of mistakes with you, Risa. I'm trying really hard not to fumble again."

"That's sweet." This time she did touch him. Her arms wound around his neck until he had to recite the alphabet to keep from tugging her close and trailing kisses over the bruise on her flat stomach. "Very sweet."

She really wasn't getting this.

When her fingers trailed down his chest and kept heading for his stomach, he put his hand over hers. Much more of that and they wouldn't talk again tonight. "I'm feeling the exact opposite of sweet right now."

She tilted her head up and he saw her sad face. The look could only be described as pity. He had no idea what that meant and he wasn't sure he liked it.

Until she spoke.

"How about we make a deal?" Her hand rested on the waistband of his pants. "Later tonight or tomorrow we'll go through the biographical information and analyze how we came to be the people we are—"

If she was trying to kill the promise made by her roaming fingers, that did it. "Can I vote we skip that part completely?"

"But for now we'll be happy we somehow survived the night, fast-forward our dating life and not worry about what all of this means."

Desire screamed through his senses. He'd never experienced a blast of longing quite like this before.

He went with honesty since chivalry failed the first time around. "It is taking every ounce of control I have left not to drag you into my bedroom, but I don't want you to have regrets."

"I can't imagine hating anything I did with you and wanting to take it back later."

"I appreciate the vote of confidence. I'm trying to figure out if it adds more pressure."

"Not to sound too forward, but I'm a sure thing." Her hand moved lower. "For you only, but definitely for you."

"If you're trying to smash my control into about a billion tiny pieces, keep saying stuff like that."

"I could come up with a nicer way to say it, maybe something more flattering to me and less desperate sounding since I really don't feel desperate, but I thought after all we've been through it might be better just to lay it out there. We had to learn something for all that running and gunning, right?"

"Definitely."

"Then I say we ignore the pleasantries and do what we want to do. You have my respect. That was earned long ago, and my feelings aren't going to suddenly disappear."

The last hold on his control snapped. "Then why are we still talking?"

Chapter Fifteen

Angie ducked into the shadows next to the brick building. Cold air whipped around her, soaking through her flannel coat and seeping deep into her bones.

The night was as wet as it was bitingly cold. The type of night when a smart person stayed inside and didn't come out until spring.

The snow came in bursts. The flurries fell thick enough to cover the ground and cloud her vision.

After everything that had happened tonight, she should be sitting in her apartment, drinking wine and being grateful she hadn't chosen the seat Mark picked first. She'd barely known the man except to fight off his halfhearted advances and read his company financial reports. Now he was dead. Killed at an office Christmas party no one wanted to go to but she insisted on holding.

She wasn't sure if the sequence of events was ironic or just tragic. Either way, she'd never look at a Christmas tree the same way again. Seeing it half burned and smashed after a one-story fall made her want to take down the fake one she'd bought for her dining room table.

She'd probably never insist on a company holiday party again, either. The infighting and complaints. The costs. And now she had to add almost being blown up and murdered to her list of items that made her holiday party insufferable.

If she were the type of person who built lasting and meaningful relationships, she might spend the evening crying and wondering what could have been. As it was, she couldn't break through the numbness filling her bones. The chill outside was nothing compared to the frigid wind blowing through her.

But she had to do something. Hours of building the worst-case scenario in her mind couldn't be worse than trying to work around the mess she'd created.

That was the only explanation for her being outside Aaron's condo after three in the morning. She'd left the police station after hours of intensive questioning and let the cab drive her around for close to twenty minutes. The keys to her apartment never left her purse.

Truth was this was not how she had envisioned the evening. If the party had gone as planned, she'd be in an expensive hotel ordering room service with Lowell. This was supposed to be their night. Even with Sonya attending the party, Lowell had bet she'd cry off early with a headache. That was how she operated. He made her do something she hated and she punished him with medical aliments.

When the night exploded, Angie had been even more convinced it would end well for her. No way would someone get the whole way to Lowell. That was just not how these things worked. So she'd seen an early night followed by a hotel.

In either scenario, she'd have Lowell and a hotel. In reality she had neither.

She'd expected a call from Lowell, but it never came. Oh, she'd made excuses at first. Brandon needed him. Lowell had to prioritize and put the public view of his family life first. It had stung, but it made sense. She was the extra piece in his life.

Still, some worry about her well-being would have been nice. They'd been sleeping together for more than a year. She was the one he turned to when he needed to complain about Brandon's activities and Sonya's craziness. When someone at work needed to be fired, she had to handle the ugly task. But when a building fell on her head, he didn't appear to care.

A quick check-in at the hospital told her Lowell had gone home. He left and never called. Didn't text or even leave a message to see if she needed him. He abandoned her the same way he had the last two women in his life.

All those hints in the conference room. The way he looked at her as he demanded to know who had launched the attack on him.

He knew and she had to cut off any attempt to pin the worst of tonight on her. There was only one person she could turn to for that, and he was upstairs with the light still on.

It took a quick check of her office contact list to even figure out where Aaron lived. She didn't have direct access to that information, but the investigation report on Aaron's company included it. Checking out his building now, she was surprised. He charged a lot for his services but lived in a relatively modest place.

Probably said something about his character. Angie never understood that. Being noble and self-sacrificing struck her as a waste of an otherwise fabulous life. With so much to buy and so many things to see and do, why settle for an everyday existence?

She flipped her collar up against the pounding wind and stepped off the curb to head across the street. She still wasn't sure what she planned to say, but she had to win him over...no matter how.

The empty street made it easy for her to cross. She'd almost reached the lobby door when two figures slipped out of the alley next door. They didn't look anywhere except at the lobby in front of them.

Something in the walk of the one on the right looked familiar. The slight limp and heavy gait. When he turned to the side to talk to his partner, even from this distance the face registered. She knew him, had spent hours trapped in a room with him. Had watched as Palmer declared him dead.

Max.

But that was impossible. He had died in that conference room. Palmer had taken his pulse and the ambulance wheeled the bodies out...or did they only take Mark's out? She couldn't remember since those shocking minutes all blurred together in her head.

Either way the only person with less right to be outside Aaron's condo than her was Max. Unless he worked for Aaron.

Her brain clicked into gear as she watched Max fiddle with the door. It opened and they disappeared inside. Without a doorman, guests should have had to buzz in. Unless they were expected.

Walking faster, she reached the building. A peek in the glass in the front door showed Max and his friend headed past the elevator. She dropped back, leaning against the side of the building as she tried to pull her thoughts together.

Her timing had been brilliant this time. She could have pushed her way upstairs and walked straight into a trap. Gone to the one person who had more to lose from last night than she did.

The rumbling pain in her stomach eased. It was if a healing light spilled through her and wiped out the panic and desperation before it could fester and grow.

Max worked for Aaron. Aaron was behind everything.

There was no other explanation. She had a new angle to work. Now she had a way to survive the scandal.

Blame Aaron.

RISA HAD INSISTED ON A shower. The hot spray of water woke her up. Her skin tingled and the bruise on her stomach quieted to a sting thanks to some aspirin. The urge to slather on the special burn cream the hospital gave her was strong, but there was nothing sexy about that smell, so she left the tube Aaron fetched for her on the counter.

Her bare toes curled into the thick carpet as she walked around his king-size bed, waiting for Aaron to pop out from his turn in the shower. They could have gone in together, but she'd wanted to scrub the grime and grit off before he touched her.

Her finger turned blue from where she'd wrapped the belt of his robe around it and pulled tight. Yeah, she wasn't nervous or anything.

"Risa?"

She spun around so fast she lost her balance. With her arm flung out to the side, she stopped herself from tripping and falling onto the bed. She sat down hard to end the comical display.

The sight of him with nothing more than a crisp white towel wrapped around his slim waist didn't help her equilibrium. If possible, his shoulders seemed even more broad without a stitch of clothing. The way his bare chest dove in a V to his muscled stomach made hers do a crazy somersault.

No wonder he ran and shot with ease. Every inch of him was physically perfect. So lethal.

Her mouth went dry.

"You okay?" His husky voice dipped into sexy territory.

Heat rushed to her cheeks. She inhaled a few times, trying to put the fire out, but the embarrassing giveaway didn't lessen.

"I'm usually more graceful than what you just saw." That wasn't true, but he could find that out on the tenth date.

He held up the burn cream tube. "I meant this."

The tightening inside her unspooled. "Oh, what about it?"

"You need to put it on."

Yeah, and after that she'd throw on a pair of panty hose because they were just as sexy. "I'm fine."

"Get on the bed." When her eyebrow raised in question, he laughed. "Not subtle, I know, but medicine before fun."

"I can think of a better order of events. I'm happy to make a list and include a description."

"I'll pass out if you do."

She pretended to check her mental list. "Fainting is not anywhere on my priority list."

He shook his head. "Point of order. Women faint."

"What do men do?"

"Drop over."

"I'm looking that up later on." And she would because that seemed like hokum to her.

"Not now." He put his hands on her shoulders and

eased her onto the bed, then squeezed some cream onto his finger.

"Definitely not now."

She sat there, thinking this had to be the least sexy start to a night that any woman had ever had.

Then his hot mouth found the sensitive bend in her neck. She leaned back to give him great access, and his lips traveled. He rained kisses across her collarbone as he untied the belt at her waist.

When she fell back across the mattress, he followed. His mouth dipped to the soft valley between her breasts as his hand found her stomach. The gentle caresses had her forgetting this was partly about doctoring her up. All she could think about was what would come after. She longed to make love to him.

Her hands wandered over his back as his fingers traced the aching skin around her injury. The raw skin soothed under his touch. When his mouth found hers again, she didn't care what he rubbed all over her.

Heat pounded off him. Energy buzzed around them until she was lost in a sensual haze of his hands and mouth.

He lifted his head. "Let me make you feel better."

"You are."

His mouth traveled over her and down the sliver of skin peeking out from the open center of her robe. When his lips brushed over her breasts and kept going, she nearly jumped out of the bed to beg him for more.

She glanced down her body. His fingers rubbed the cream in soft circles over her injury while his mouth inflamed the rest of her. The mix of delicate touches and his hungry mouth proved to be the hottest foreplay she could imagine.

When he dropped the cream container on the floor, she pulled him back up to face her. "Thank you."

"We're not done yet." He rolled to his back, taking her with him. "I think you'll be more comfortable in this position this time around. No pressure on the stomach."

Her legs straddled his trim hips. His impressive erection pressed against her as she cradled him, teasing and preparing them both for what was to come.

He reached over and grabbed the condom off the nightstand. All traces of exhaustion had left his face. His eyes glowed with a vibrant desire as his hands skated over her.

"I don't want to be done." She kissed his chin, then his neck when he lifted his head higher. "I want to burn. Make me burn for you."

His mouth closed over hers, and her body caught fire. She felt the tug at her waist then the robe fell open. Every cell caught fire as his hands roamed over her. The brush of his fingertips. The sure touch as he found a spot that had her head falling forward.

Her breath jammed in her chest as his palms landed on the back of her thighs and pressed her closer. She felt him enter, gasped as his body stretched and inflamed her. She wanted to talk, to whisper his name, but instinct took over. Her body moved, slow and steady until he took over the rhythm and everything inside her tightened.

Then she couldn't think at all.

Chapter Sixteen

An hour later, Aaron still couldn't sleep. Thoughts and possibilities pinged around his brain. He'd taken all the pieces apart from Elan and still couldn't get any of them to fit back together in a logical way.

When he wasn't thinking about strategies and plotting, his mind wandered to Risa. The smooth skin and expert hands.

Yeah, if this level of work and personal life continued, he didn't foresee a decent night's sleep in a very long time.

He bent his arm behind his head and wrapped the other arm around Risa. She lay naked and curled up on his side, her light breathing blowing across his hypersensitive skin.

This he could get used to.

She'd been as free and giving in bed as he'd fantasized she'd be. With her mouth and her hands, she'd zapped his strength and then refilled it. She wrapped around him until all he could feel or see or smell was her.

The hours of violence that had preceded the session in the bedroom hadn't cooled his desire for her one bit. If anything, by the time he got her to safety he'd wanted to rip her clothes off and push deep inside her. Probably not very heroic on his part, but she didn't complain when he did just that.

Neither did he. The lovemaking session relaxed his muscles and fed a need that had been brewing inside him for longer than he would have guessed. He toyed with the reason he'd failed to call her back for another date a week ago.

He had all sorts of excuses about being busy and concentrating on the Craft problem. The reality was being with her like this made it hard to imagine being anywhere else. The last time he'd walked down that road he'd ended up alone, watching the couch he'd owned for years get loaded into his ex's moving van. Not exactly an event he wanted to repeat.

"Why aren't you sleeping?" Risa's mumbled question vibrated against his bare chest.

The sound of her voice wiped out all memories of Pam and their train wreck of a relationship. It almost knocked out the nagging questions about what had happened tonight at the conference center. Almost.

"Still on edge, I guess. It's hard to turn the adrenaline off once it starts pumping." And his mind took even longer.

She treated him to a fake half snore, half grunt. "I could sleep for a month."

"I am all for staying in bed, if that is the offer you're making." His hand slipped down to her lower back and the soft skin he'd kissed so many times just an hour before. "Or is that not what you meant?"

"You wore me out with an hour. If I stayed here I'd need medical attention."

She balanced on her elbow and stared down at him. With her forefinger, she traced a pattern over and around his nipple.

Even in the dark bedroom he could see the flash of her smile. Talking with her, watching her face light up, calmed the frustration gnawing at the edges of his brain.

"Just what every man wants to hear."

"Then you should be delirious." She dropped a nibbling kiss on his chest.

"Much more of that and we'll need to find more condoms."

"Tomorrow." She snuggled closer, with her long hair fanning over him.

He ran his fingers through the strands, feeling the ends still damp from her shower. "I'm going to hold you to that."

"Can we just agree tonight was the worst holiday party ever? I mean, like epically bad."

He laughed until his muscles ached. It took a small pinch to his biceps to get him to focus again. "Any chance you'll still hold yours there?"

She lifted her leg in the air behind her and twisted her ankle around in circles. Watching the move made his twisted knee throb in pain.

"Since we were hoping for an indoor venue and Elan is now open air, I kind of doubt it." Even she laughed this time, causing her body to vibrate against him.

"Sorry."

"You didn't blow it up or let in the bad guys or cause any one of a hundred of the odd things that happened tonight." Her leg stopped moving. "We still don't know who did, do we?"

"Not yet. The fire marshal will do an investigation. The bomb components were crude and not well hidden, so I don't think this will take too long."

"That's probably good for Elan."

"I doubt they see it that way, but the owners want

the conference center up and running fast, and that will require a closed investigation and insurance money."

She let her leg fall back to the mattress. "Any more information on Craft's son and Royal?"

Aaron reached over and grabbed his cell off the nightstand. He'd already read the text an hour ago but wanted to double-check. He was desperate to hear good news about Royal and kept asking for details until Gail joked about needing sleep.

He clicked a few buttons. "The last report from Gail was that Brandon was still not responding but the doctors were hopeful. Royal has moved into the bitching phase of his recovery where he insists on going home immediately and coming to work tomorrow."

"At least the part about Royal is good to hear."

It was the best news, actually. Aaron appreciated Royal more with every assignment.

Risa yawned and Aaron closed his eyes on the hope sleep might finally come. Her husky voice had him opening them again.

"Tell me about their marriage."

Aaron turned the alarm clock to face him. The bright green numbers showed a time that couldn't possibly be right...could it?

The hours had flipped by and his eyes still stayed open. It was like some sick cosmic joke. "Now?"

"Talking will help you sleep."

Aaron had no idea how that was possible, but he was enjoying the intimacy, so he didn't argue. "They got married at nineteen. He told me once he would have married her right out of high school but he worried people would think they *had* to get married."

Risa's shoulders shook on a new round of laughter. "That would be terrible, I guess."

"Apparently it was pretty normal for where he grew up and he wanted to act a different way." Aaron scooted down on the bed to fit his body closer against hers. "He went into the army, got out and threw in with me. For the most part, he seems satisfied with the life he picked."

"You sound skeptical."

"It works for him. Wife and kids aren't really my thing." Aaron said the last words as part of an automatic loop. He'd repeated the refrain so many times that it now came out without any thought.

"You're antimarriage?"

Talk about a conversation he never wanted to have again. "My dad would probably like grandkids but I tried the marriage thing once and only got as far as the engagement. She left."

Risa scoffed. "So?"

He froze. "What do you mean, so?"

"One woman broke your heart and now you swear you'll never love again?" She snorted.

She couldn't make her view clearer than that. "You're making a lot of noises all of a sudden."

"Sounds to me like a bad country music song."

He almost laughed at her choice of words. "I think I expected more sympathy."

She lifted her head and stared him down. Her eyes penetrated the darkness and bored right into him. "My boyfriend took all my money and more than a little of my pride. He ruined my credit. By the time his butt hit the skids, I was in huge financial trouble."

Whatever amusement he felt fled. The idea of Risa with some loser made him ready to punch someone. "This is the guy who lied?"

"Yes, and you don't see me writing off the entire male population in response. After all, I think we learned tonight that life is too short and too risky to waste on thinking negatively all the time."

Aaron ignored the lecture and went to the topic most on his mind. "Where is this guy?"

"Long gone and he's judgment-proof, so don't bother." She glanced at the window and held there as if mesmerized by the snow blowing under the streetlights.

Aaron had other things on his mind. "I can still track him down and hit him."

"Just that you offered is enough." She rubbed her palm over his chest, then kissed the area she'd caressed. "And, really, I'd rather you just admit that not all women are disposable."

"I know I never said that."

"You sure?"

"I'm not an idiot, first of all. But I don't believe it, either. You're not interchangeable or whatever word you used." He searched his mind for any woman he'd switch with her, and every cell inside him rebelled at the idea. He couldn't even go there.

"But you like to keep things light."

The warning light flashed. Nothing good waited in the direction of that conversation. "How did we get on this subject?"

"What would you rather talk about?" She lifted herself up higher off his body, then suddenly stilled. "Was that a knock? Now?"

He was moving before she finished the question. He flipped the covers off him and started for the door.

"You should put on some pants."

He stopped in midstride and changed direction. "Good idea. Easier to hide the gun."

"That's totally not what I meant."

He turned and pointed at her. "In the bathroom and

do not come out. Take the phone with you in case you need to call 911."

"It could be something else."

"I doubt it."

Chapter Seventeen

As soon as Aaron left the room, Risa jumped off the bed. She scanned the room and then went to the credenza under the window. Opening the top drawer, then the second, she rummaged through the stacks of folded clothes and found exactly what she needed.

Grabbing her underwear from the chair, she slid them on. Next came the pair of his boxers she borrowed. The makeshift shorts slipped when she walked, so she rolled the waist to make them tighter. A sweatshirt from the floor that fell to her knees and the gun he had tucked in the nightstand while she watched completed the outfit.

She slipped her cell next to the gun in the elastic band of her panties and slipped into the hall to check on Aaron. A light by the television cast a soft glow on the room. She could hear the pounding of a fist from the hall and the incessant chime of the bell.

Whoever this was didn't honor the idea of nighttime privacy. He also didn't understand that making a lot of noise in a condo complex guaranteed numerous calls to the police.

Right now nothing much was happening. Aaron stood to the side of the front door wearing nothing more than a pair of jeans.

"What do you want?" His muffled voice traveled

down the hallway to her. "Whatever it is can wait until tomorrow."

Control oozed off him and anger edged his voice. Whatever he saw had him steadying his stance and tensing his shoulders. She knew from experience that could not be good.

She couldn't hear what the visitor said, but it must have satisfied Aaron because he unlocked the door. The knob twisted next.

When she saw a guy walk in—a guy she recalled from the incident at Elan—she figured he was one of Aaron's men. She missed that Aaron hadn't lowered his weapon until she got halfway down the hall toward them. By then it was too late to turn around and pretend she wasn't there.

The guy was thirty-something with dark hair. He shared the same lethal look as Aaron but had the benefit of being fully clothed. If the puffed-out chest was any indication, the visitor also wore a protective vest. Aaron didn't even wear a shirt.

As if sensing her presence behind him, the guy turned and nodded in her direction. "Ma'am."

Aaron barely spared her a glance, but his furious expression said everything she needed to know. This guy, whoever he was, was not a friend.

"Go back in the bedroom." Aaron motioned as he spoke.

The guy held up a hand. "Wait a second. This impacts her, too. She was at the conference center."

She ran through every memory of the past day, trying to recall one of him. Nothing came to her.

The end of the night was a haze of emergency responders and explosion debris. A parade of people passed by her, some from the Elan Conference Center and others from Craft and medical services. After a few seconds all the faces except those of Royal and Aaron blended together.

She gave up and asked what she wanted to know. "Who are you?"

Aaron pressed his hand against the door and flipped it shut. With his gun up, he walked the other man deeper into the living room. "This is Max. He works for Palmer, the Craft head of security."

The name tickled a memory free. "Someone said you were dead."

"Apparently not."

Aaron shifted until he stood in front of Max. "Why are you here?"

Max smiled as he nodded at Aaron's gun. "Are you going to lower that?"

"No."

The smile disappeared as fast as it came. Max increased his stance, balancing his feet apart and keeping his hands at his sides. "I have some information you need for the investigation."

"Bring it to my office tomorrow. This is unacceptable."

"It's an emergency."

"I think we've had enough of those for one evening."

Something in Aaron's tone had Risa backing up. She stopped when her bare calves hit the chair by the sliding glass door. She wished she'd put on pants and a bra. Her current outfit made her feel even more vulnerable than the hulking intruder.

"Tell me what is so important that you need to be here at this hour." The question was casual, but the way Aaron handled the gun was anything but.

Max reached beneath his vest. "Could we—"

Aaron snapped. "Do not move."

"You're not very appreciative."

"I'm trying to figure out how you know where I live."

Max shrugged. "Craft had Palmer do a check. I looked in the file. It was pretty simple."

"How enterprising of you."

While the men postured, she slipped her leg on the chair's armrest and balanced there. The gun at the small of her back itched and the cell migrated past the elastic band of her underwear.

After a moment of tense silence, Max exhaled. "The person behind this—the kidnap attempt, the threats and the bombing—is Brandon."

To Risa's memory the kid was one of the most seriously injured in the blast. If he was the attacker he wasn't very competent. Aaron had made that argument to her just a few hours ago.

And he didn't look any more impressed with the supposed big revelation now. "Tell the police."

"No one will believe me."

"Why should I?"

"I'm here to help." Max shook his head before making another grab at his vest. "Let me show you—"

Aaron closed in. "I said, don't move."

Max screwed up his lips in a frown. "Then we'll do this the hard way."

The glass door to the balcony behind her shattered. One minute it was there and the next the glass fell to the floor and the freezing winter wind blew in. Lost in the surreal moment, frozen to her spot, she didn't move.

A second man jumped into the room and came right for her. Held a gun and had huge hands. They reached for her, heading straight for her head.

"Risa, move!"

She ducked and spun, trying to get out of the second guy's line of attack. She'd almost made it when he grabbed her sweatshirt. Bunching it in his fist, he choked her as he pulled her back.

She fell against the guy's side as his meaty hand clamped down on her neck. Glancing up, she saw Aaron had barely moved. He stood in the same place with his gun aimed at Max's head.

Max sat still, not even trying to run or reach for a gun. "That was fun."

The light hit the sweat across Aaron's shoulders. "Let her go or I kill Max," he said to the gunman holding her.

"That's not going to happen."

Aaron closed the distance between him and Max. "I don't miss at this range."

"Let me tell you what's going to happen," Max said.

"You are going to lower the weapon and leave. We'll deal with the rest tomorrow."

"I don't see that happening." Max crossed his legs, looking every bit as content as a guy finishing a big meal at an expensive restaurant. If the weapon in his face scared him, he did a heck of a job hiding it.

Risa was having a harder time. Being under the gun again had her insides shaking hard.

Aaron shot the second attacker another look. "Lower the gun."

Max talked over him. "You and your girlfriend are going to die in a home invasion. Something brutal and quick, though not as quick as you might like. We just need to keep the screaming to a minimum, but there are ways to do that."

"That will be a bit suspect after everything we've already been through tonight, don't you think?" Aaron returned.

Max acted as if he was weighing the choices. "Did I forget to mention you'll be blamed for the bombing? Yes, see, you had a falling-out with Lowell and found out he planned to fire you, which he is about to do."

"And you'll make the evidence trace back to me."

Risa's heart slammed against her rib cage. It knocked so hard she couldn't believe they couldn't hear the thumping.

She swallowed hard and forced her mind to focus. The plan sounded like nonsense to her. Aaron had a gun and Max just sat there.

When Aaron didn't make a move, Max continued. "In your fury, you came up with a plan to destroy Lowell and Craft Industries, but it backfired. Then one of the men you hired to help you turned on you and killed you both."

Aaron shook his head. "There are so many flaws with that plan. No police officer will accept it. Most high school crime clubs could reason that one through."

Max shrugged. "We'll fix it later."

She saw heat flare in Aaron's eyes when he heard the "we" in Max's remark. She guessed it was a slip that meant something.

"Sorry, ma'am, but your poor taste in men is to blame for your death." Max's gaze took a trip over her body. "If it's any consolation, we waited until you two were done in the bedroom to make a play."

Her stomach rolled as bile rushed up her throat. She would have doubled over and thrown up if the guy behind her hadn't held her in place.

Something so personal, so private, and these disgusting creatures had watched. She wanted to jump in the shower and scrub until a layer of skin peeled off.

Max looked up at Aaron. "Nice moves, by the way."

"You didn't see anything."

"True, but you two are very noisy."

The rolling and pitching didn't stop. Knowing they might not have seen the intimacy that meant so much to her did not make the horror of the situation any less potent.

"Now, it's time." Max put his hands on the armrests as if he was going to stand.

Aaron was on him in a second. "Did you miss the fact that I'm holding a gun?"

Max shot out of the chair. The diving tackle hit Aaron in the stomach and sent him flying back and into the wall. A punch to the jaw followed, then one to the gut. Aaron took it all as Max pulled a gun out of his jacket.

When Aaron bent over, Risa feared the exhaustion and injuries had piled up to take him out of the fight early. Max's smile turned feral when he lifted his arm to slam his gun down on Aaron's head.

At the last second Aaron shifted and then rammed a knee into Max's stomach that had him coughing. A whack with the gun across the jaw knocked him sideways and Aaron took advantage by nailing Max with a flexed kick to the kneecap.

Max squealed in pain but stayed upright. Both men grunted and landed additional punches.

Through it all, the man behind her just stood there. He held her neck in a pinch that squeezed a nerve and sent a surge of pain radiating up and down her spine. Risa could only guess the guy was so sure of his hold that he didn't bother to search her for a gun.

Even now her oversize sweatshirt hid her greatest weapon, the gun Aaron had given her the confidence to fire.

When Aaron took out Max's injured leg and knocked

him to the floor, she got ready to make her move. She knew if Aaron got the upper hand, the second guy would retaliate with a bullet.

She couldn't allow a gunfire bloodbath. At this range, they would both fire and go down and leave her standing there.

As Aaron lifted his gun, so did the second attacker. Risa didn't hesitate. She whipped out her weapon. The waves of fear rattling her back teeth threw off her aim. The gun shook in her hands and she fired as she yanked free.

The shot hit the leg of the guy holding her and sent him slamming to the floor. His gun dropped with him and she kicked it under the couch.

The swearing and the gunshot had Max and Aaron spinning in her direction as someone pounded on the wall from the condo next to them.

Aaron's mouth dropped open as his gaze slid to the man on the floor, then back to her face. In that beat of hesitation, Max made his move. He slipped his gun out of the holder at his waist and with lightning speed he fired. Aaron jumped on him, but it was too late.

The shot slammed into Max's partner and dropped him without a noise. It was brutal and final and it didn't make any sense. Her brain froze as it fought to register the change in direction of the chaos in the room. She kept breathing, waiting for some part of her body to ache and the blood to appear.

But Max didn't go after her. Neither did he shoot Aaron. And that split decision had the room reeling. Everything tilted and nothing moved.

"No loose ends." Then Max was on his feet and running.

He headed for the balcony door while she and Aaron

watched in joint confusion. Max bolted in front of them before they could lift their arms to stop him.

Hooking a piece of metal from his belt to the balcony railing, Max started to leap over the side. The move was so unexpected, she could only stand there, rooted to the floor.

Aaron, however, reacted immediately. He lunged forward and caught Max in midair. The flight and speed pulled them both into the rail with a loud clank. A neighbor shouted for quiet and the surreal moment was not lost on Risa.

Aaron's strength unleashed like a raging beast, allowing him to perform the impossible. A nearly one-armed diving catch of a hundred-eighty-pound male. He grunted as Max's full weight pulled him down into the dark night, but he wrestled and tugged, never losing his grip on Max.

The odds were so unrealistic that she doubted anyone would ever believe the story.

The sight sent a punch of energy to her fatigued legs. She ran out and wrapped her arms around Aaron's waist to give him leverage. Together they forced Max back over the railing. Gravity brought both men crashing to the cement patio.

Fueled by a fighting fury Risa couldn't imagine, Aaron straddled Max and leaned down with a hand on his throat. "Now we can talk."

Chapter Eighteen

Angie huddled in the cold, staring up at the line of windows she knew belonged to Aaron's condo. A light burned bright against the sheer curtain and shadows moved just inside.

If possible, the temperature had dropped another twenty degrees in the past few minutes. The waiting only highlighted the lack of amenities. For not the first time tonight, she wished she'd waited until spring to do this. At least then it would be warm if she had to roam around outside.

Max and his buddy had gone up over an hour ago. In the darkness she saw moving shadows and heard bangs she thought might be gunfire. She waited for the the sight of Aaron catapulting out of a window but it never came.

Much more of this wait for a final word and her feet would freeze to the pavement. She'd dressed for a party and changed only when the hospital personnel had insisted. The hospital scrubs and stylish black work pumps didn't do anything to keep her warm.

She shifted her position, trying to keep the blood flowing through her exhausted body. The inactivity had the muscles in her legs seizing up. Standing was tough, but a few more minutes and walking might prove impossible.

She knew she should go home and let the men fight this out. Whatever play she had left, she'd have to wait and see what Aaron and Max had planned. See who survived. If Max won, and she suspected he would since he had the element of surprise on his side, she stood a chance of turning this around. Max was young and handsome. There would be worse things than convincing him to look the other way over something that amounted to nothing.

But she couldn't walk away just yet. The idea that someone was playing a game right under her nose, in the office she ran with precision, filled her with fury. The heated anger might be the only thing staving off hyperthermia at the moment.

"You can give up for the night and go to bed."

She froze at the sound of the familiar male voice behind her. She turned and saw Palmer leaning against a sedan just a few feet away from her. The car wasn't his, but he looked comfortable borrowing it.

Always fashionable, even in his security garb, he wore the wool camel-colored coat he brought to the office each day. No gloves or hat. No sign of freezing out there like a normal person.

She'd never heard him approach, and now her mind scrambled to place him in the area at this time of night. He didn't live in this part of Virginia, but neither did she.

"Palmer?" She recognized him, but her mind wanted confirmation.

He unfolded his arms and pushed off the car. In two steps he stood next to her, staring up at the condo building. "I took care of it for you. You have no worries and there is nothing else you can do tonight. Trust me."

She blinked, trying so hard to focus on what he was saying. "I don't understand."

"You can go back home." He held a hand up toward the condo. "This is out of your hands now. In some ways, it's out of mine. Everything has been put in motion and all we can do now I live with the consequences."

Reality smacked into her. This could be some sort of test, some way to get her to admit to what she had done into a hidden recording device. She'd seen enough television programs to know this could be a setup, and by talking she'd be the one to buy her way into jail. She wouldn't need Aaron's or anyone else's help on that path to self-destruction.

Playing it cool was the answer. She excelled at control and called on her vast reserve one more time tonight. "I don't know what you're talking about."

"You are standing outside Aaron McBain's home at—" Palmer glanced at his watch. "Three in the morning. Can that be right? Have we really lost the entire evening and most of the early morning? The police took longer than anyone expected. Who knew so many questions could lead to so many wrong answers?"

"I'm out because I needed to clear my head."

Palmer frowned at her. "At least be original with your lies. This is not a story you could sell to anyone."

The pretense slipped. Part of her wanted to shout at him until he told her what was going on. After all, if she was here to check on McBain, that probably meant Palmer was, too.

"Since you're so big on alibis and plausible stories, what are you doing here?"

"Same as you. Cleaning up loose ends." He looked around before his gaze came back to land on her. "See? Simple is always better."

She had no idea what to say to that. Anything she said could implicate her. "I should leave."

She turned on her heel. She picked a random direction and started walking.

"You asked the wrong man in the office for help."

At Palmer's words she stopped. With a slow turn, she spun around to face him again. "What are you talking about?"

"Max is young but he knew enough to know you wanted to do something very naughty and he came to me out of concern."

She cursed her luck. Her radar for the right man to use for the job rarely misfired.

"You talked in cryptic terms, and my man was not as intelligent as I had hoped, but I got the overall scheme. At first I considered going to Lowell, then figured it wouldn't do any good. He's always had a soft spot for you. There's a reason you've lasted so much longer than any of the others."

"He does?"

"Rather than let you launch it, I stepped in and chose the guys to help you. I controlled it all."

She didn't pretend he misunderstood or had the wrong person. Not now that she knew who had been pulling the strings all night. The same person who almost killed them all with a mistimed bomb. "Why?"

"You wanted to scare Lowell. That was the plan, right? Make him think you needed him, put him in a tough position. Use the situation to test his love or grab some cash."

"You're wrong." But he wasn't. He'd worked through the riddle and figured it all out.

"But your timing was off and McBain and that

woman just happened to get off on the wrong floor. What were the chances of that?"

She'd been asking herself the same question since she saw McBain get on that elevator. "But you had something bigger planned for the party. I may have been testing Lowell, but you were way ahead of me. Why?"

"That is none of your business."

"You tried to…hurt him." She didn't want to say the actual words. If she accused Palmer of trying to kill Lowell, she ran the risk of him taking her out right there on the street. Better for him to think she admired his work.

"I used the resources you were putting in place. Your presence gave me a potential fall guy, or fall gal, as you will."

There it was. She sensed any investigation would highlight her role. She was an obvious suspect and she feared there was evidence she'd never touched but that pointed to her.

"But why?" she asked because she couldn't make that piece of the puzzle fit.

"My issues with Lowell Craft are my own."

And she could analyze that later. Getting out of this became her only goal. She would do anything. "So, now what?"

Palmer glanced at McBain's condo. "I found someone else to blame."

"You might be kidding yourself. He is a smart guy. People know that he left the party to hunt down killers in the building, and he has the bodies to prove it."

"Bodies I chose for you and who will not tell tales or trace back to any trouble. You're welcome, by the way."

"I'm supposed to be grateful you turned my plan into

a catastrophe? I'm almost afraid to ask what you have planned for McBain."

"Tomorrow at the office we'll be mourning Aaron's death as another burglary-homicide statistic."

AARON SHUT THE DOOR TO the condo and locked it behind him. Convincing two neighbors the noise meant nothing took longer than he expected. Between the broken glass and the gunfire, they were convinced of a break-in. Since they were essentially correct, he didn't talk them out of it. Instead, he talked around it.

The last thing he needed was the police riding in and questioning Max before Aaron could get any helpful information. One step into the police station and this guy would call a lawyer. The information train would stop then, and Aaron couldn't let that happen. He needed help, and this guy was in the perfect position to offer it.

Not that anyone missed him back here.

Max sat bound and gagged on a chair. Risa stood a few feet away, unmoving except for an occasional blink and her steady breathing. She held a gun like a pro and Aaron couldn't figure out how he felt about that change.

He wanted her free and innocent. Knowing him shouldn't shift her life that drastically. Right now he had to believe she wore a mask. The emotion he saw didn't match the woman he knew.

He guessed that her insides were crumbling at the thought of a dead guy lying nearly at her feet. She hadn't killed him, but blood had flooded all over her the past twenty-four hours. The way she picked up the gun showed spirit, but the way she almost dropped it reflected the real her. She should never touch one outside of a shooting range or sporting club.

He ached with the need to put her back in the coffee

shop, chuckling at silly internet sites. But she did slide right into the kick-butt role and his life with ease. That he would have to assess later, if he could find a moment when someone wasn't trying to kill him.

Aaron lifted his arm, trying to work out the kinks and muscle strain. Next time he'd let the guy sail over the balcony and skip the bruised shoulder.

Dropping into the seat directly across from Max, Aaron took out his gun and balanced it on his lap. The move bordered on dramatic, but he liked the feel of threatening a guy who didn't think twice about threatening Risa.

Aaron leaned forward. "Do you know why I'm letting you live?" Max was gagged, but he didn't even so much as blink, so Aaron continued. "Because you're going to tell me who hired you."

Max shook his head. Disappointment kicked Aaron in the gut. He'd hoped this would be smooth and easy. He wasn't sure why that would be the case since nothing else in this case had gone like that, but a guy could hope. Especially when what he really wanted to do was climb back into bed with the woman standing over his shoulder.

Aaron removed the gag. "You yell or try to move and I'll shoot you in the head. Don't doubt that I will."

"You aren't the type."

"You are sadly mistaken. A man pushed to the edge can do many things he never thought possible. And killing a kid like you was never that far out of my range to begin with."

"You don't understand."

"That's right. Now it's your turn to talk."

"I don't know anything. I did what I was told and pocketed the cash. There's no trail to anyone."

Aaron dropped back in his chair amazed at how much information the kid volunteered. Apparently no one told him that sort of thing was a dead giveaway. Whenever anyone used ten words to say two, the thing buried underneath was worth digging up.

"See, that's the wrong answer. The same answer that gets you killed."

Max's gaze traveled from Risa to Aaron and back again. "I'm unarmed."

"But you're not innocent, are you?" Risa dropped that gem.

Aaron knew her mind had gone back to the comment about having an audience for their lovemaking. That one made him want to spit, but he guessed a woman would really take offense.

He gave Max a man-to-man look. "You shouldn't have mentioned the bedroom thing."

He shook his head. "I didn't see anything."

Risa snorted. "A few minutes ago you were all about describing it and making me feel uncomfortable. It's too late to change that story now."

"I didn't mean—"

"And you're a sick puppy."

"Max, here's what you need to understand." Aaron slid his hand over his gun, highlighting the weapon for Max without saying a word about it. "No prosecutor would bring charges for your death after what we've been through tonight. A home invasion on the night of a newsworthy attack is only going to end in sympathy for us. Big sympathy."

"But I'm unarmed," Max repeated.

"You won't be when I'm done." Aaron had Max's gun secured. Aaron had never planted a gun after the fact in his life and he was not going to start now, but the kid didn't need to know the particulars. Just because he didn't have a conscience didn't mean Aaron didn't. "Between the evidence that already exists and the stuff I plan to plant, it won't take a genius to tie you to the bombing."

Risa leaned against Aaron's chair. "And then you're in huge trouble."

There was some comfort knowing he could say this stuff, that she would back him up without rehearsing, but that he didn't have to rush later to explain. She got that this was a bit. She was not someone who would do and say these things for real. She took it in stride as he poured on the acting, too.

Max continued to stare at both of them.

He must have decided Risa was the softer pitch because he aimed his new set of pleas at her. "Ma'am, please."

"She's not going to help you." Aaron knew that down to his bones. Max had taken the wrong tact. He'd been one more guy to take a shot at her on a day when her patience was blown.

Big mistake.

"She's done having men grab her. I know I could go a nice long while before I see it again." Just the thought of it made the top of his head blow off.

"I didn't touch her"

"Your friend did. Not sexually, but he put his hands on her and scared her. And then there's the part where you promised to kill her. So let's try this again." Aaron decided to up the ante.

He'd never kill a man for the joy of killing, though it was tempting tonight. No matter how much he might want to be that guy, he wasn't. He played by the rules. He'd entered the security field because he truly believed people had a right to feel safe in their lives and he wanted to provide that safety.

"Please, I can't say anything."

Aaron almost rolled his eyes. Gone was the tough guy who sat in the chair and tormented Risa with mental images she wouldn't soon forget. He'd silently dared them to touch him. He was whining like a baby now.

"Begging isn't the answer, Max. You just need to tell me the truth."

"You don't understand."

"I'm getting tired of him saying that," she mumbled.

Aaron agreed. To bring a quicker end to the game, he borrowed a strategy from Lowell. If that idiot could make people jump, surely Aaron could do the same. After all, he had three weapons within two feet of him. That had to be an encouragement of some sort for Max.

Aaron fingered the trigger. "You have five seconds to give me a name."

"Or?" The snotty tone had disappeared. This one sounded more like a kid ready to pee his pants.

Good. "You won't live to hear six."

"I… But…"

"You're going to tell me what you know and then you're going to make a call to your boss and say I'm dead."

"If I don't?"

"I promise to call an ambulance for you." Risa hesitated a beat to the perfect effect. "Eventually."

Chapter Nineteen

Angie sat by herself on one side of Lowell's big black desk. He hadn't looked up or even acknowledged her presence since his secretary ushered her inside.

The office buzz said everyone had been interviewed and accounted for. Mark was the only recorded death and there would be a memorial service for him later that week and a funeral in a state far away, held by people she didn't know.

Brandon would be home from the hospital in a few days and Sonya had already called thirteen times. The number would likely double by noon. She was a worrier, but this time she had reason.

For the first time ever, Angie felt a twinge of sympathy for the other woman. But Angie felt worse for her predicament. Sonya would get her hair done and be fine. Angie had to deal with the numbing possibility of a criminal record.

No one thought the incident had changed Lowell. Changing him was impossible. When his old secretary had died, a woman he'd spent hours with each day for a decade, Lowell had taken off exactly one hour. That was his mourning for a special woman in his life.

She knew all the stories, but since she hadn't heard one word from him since they left the center, she thought something had shifted. Their relationship had ended. His silent declaration of the same was clear as he signed paperwork in silence.

After a sleepless night and a morning filled with enough dread to keep her in the bathroom throwing up, she wanted this part over. Palmer had assured her he'd taken care of it. Despite wanting to hang around McBain's condo last night, she'd left when Palmer told her to. Actually she'd stayed out of sight in the parking lot hoping for more information or at least a hint of what happened, but it never came.

Trusting his word without more proof seemed impossible. His betrayal of Lowell made hers look like a schoolgirl joke. Depending on Palmer now to get her out of this mess seemed foolish. But what choice did she have?

After a single knock, the betrayer in question walked in. Palmer donned his security blazer and gray flannel pants. She wondered how many of those uniforms he owned because the one from yesterday wasn't good for anything but the trash can anymore. This one looked exactly the same, even shared the same crease marks.

Palmer stepped up to the desk but didn't sit down. He stood in his usual stance with his hands linked behind his back. It managed to be both threatening and deferential.

"Sir, there is a situation we need to discuss. I am afraid it is of some urgency and can't be put off until a later meeting even though it's not on your agenda."

Angie's heart jumped to her throat and lodged there. This was it. The double cross that would end with her in jail.

Lowell kept signing. "Go ahead."

"While necessary, it also is of some delicacy. Perhaps

we should discuss it first and then see if it is something you wish to share with staff."

Palmer waited, but Lowell didn't stop working. "Today, Palmer."

Stress pulled across Palmer's cheeks. "Very well. I know you wished to comb through the details of last evening. Specifically, you were looking for clarity on the McBain situation."

"You are using a lot of words to say whatever it is you're trying to say. Get to it."

"I received some terrible news earlier this morning about McBain."

Hope sailed around the room. With those few words, Angie felt a curtain of tension lift. The debilitating fear stopped pounding her. While the world didn't shift back into control, there was a path back to normalcy.

She didn't have the time or inclination to mourn McBain. His snooping had caused this, caused every bad thing that had happened. With him gone, the office would run as it had before. If she was lucky and bided her time, she might even work her way back into Lowell's good graces.

She had the perfect slinky negligee to make that happen. Even Palmer admitted she was a favorite. Someone in her position knew how to stay there. They could ride out this bump….

She'd insist they did.

Lowell finally lowered his pen and leaned back in his big chair. Like everything else in the office, it was oversize and made solely for his comfort. "What are you talking about? You are talking in circles and making grand statements. What exactly is the issue with Aaron?"

"I'm afraid there was an accident involving Aaron

and his girlfriend. A case of being in the wrong place at the wrong time, though they didn't cause this. All they were doing was sleeping and the condo was robbed."

Angie fought back the urge to smile. She bit the inside of her cheek to keep any amusement from showing on her face. This wasn't the time for glee.

Lowell frowned as he glanced out the huge window behind his desk. Snow fell heavy now. From this floor, they could see the Christmas lights and garland in the courtyard of the building.

He turned back to them with a blank expression on his face. "When?"

"Last night. The wounds were fatal."

Lowell tapped his pen against his open hand. "It wasn't in the paper."

"I, uh…" Palmer verbally faltered, but his outward appearance never changed. "The news likely came well after the deadline."

"And you know it from whom?"

"A source at the police station. He owed me a favor and knew about my previous check on McBain."

"Hmm." Lowell continued to play with his pen, twisting it between his fingers and stopping only to tap the end against his desk.

She'd never seen him play with the things around him like that before. He wasn't a man in constant movement. He could sit for hours, poring over reports or analyzing documents.

Palmer hesitated, the confusion obvious in his frown and pursed lips. "While this sort of thing is not your preferred activity, we could make memorial arrangements. Once Mark's service is behind us, of course. I have no idea about the girlfriend, but that should be easy enough information to track down."

"Sure."

"Okay, then." Palmer looked at her, then at Lowell.

He understood the discomfort. The longer this conversation dragged on, the more her confidence faltered. What had started out as a flash of great news was turning into a cryptic talk that had her stomach churning.

"I'll leave you." Palmer got the whole way to the door before Lowell stopped him.

"One thing." With the utmost care, Lowell placed the pen on his desk blotter. "I believe your information is faulty."

Her heart's roller-coaster ride speed up. One minute relief lifted her up and the next despair dragged her down.

Palmer didn't move. "Excuse me?"

"None of this is true."

"Why do you say that?"

"I talked with Aaron ten minutes ago."

"That's not possible."

The bathroom door on the right side of the room opened and Aaron and the woman Angie guessed was his girlfriend slipped out. They looked surprisingly rested and very much alive.

Lowell nodded in welcome. "Aaron."

Angie's mind spun, refusing to land on a logical space. "Who is this?"

Aaron shifted his weight until he stood slightly in front of the woman. The protective posture was clear. He would throw down for her against any of them.

"Risa Peters, the woman who was nearly kidnapped twice." He glanced at her. "Is that the right number?"

She closed one eye as if thinking the ridiculous question through. "I think it was actually three times. Four if you count last night, but that was more like a murder attempt."

Aaron waved the comment off. "Technically, that's a different thing."

Palmer shut the office door again and took up his position next to the desk. "What are you two talking about?"

"Oh, I'm sorry. I thought I was clear." Aaron brushed his hand down Risa's arm. "This is the woman your men tried to grab when they were supposed to grab Angie."

She ran through a visual checklist. Small breasts. Too-dark hair. A corn-fed country look. This Risa person looked nothing like her. "That's nonsense."

Risa shrugged. "If it's any consolation, I don't think we look alike, either."

"Of course not." Aaron winked at her. "I much prefer you."

"Thanks." Risa looked pleased at the idea, though Angie did not know how that was possible.

Palmer shifted position until he hovered near the side of the desk, aligned with Lowell. It was a physical as well as verbal show of loyalty. "I don't know what you're doing here. This is not a game. People died yesterday."

The amusement faded from Aaron's face. "And one more died last night. And if you keep playing this game and covering your tracks, I don't know how many more reports we'll have to make to the police. The good news is we probably won't destroy another conference center."

"Who else died?" Lowell asked.

"Remember Max?"

Lowell paged through the paperwork on the edge of his desk. "He died at the center. Palmer took his pulse and delivered the bad news. That was the report, Mark and Max."

Angie knew when to jump off a train. "I remember that. It was both of them."

"Well, then, Max miraculously rose from the dead. Trust me, I know because he showed up at my place ready to stage a home-invasion-style murder early this morning." Aaron's furious glare shot to Palmer. "That was on your orders, right? Kill me. Kill Risa. After some work, the evidence would have pointed to me. Problem is, it wouldn't have ended there. My partner would have picked up the charge, knowing I wasn't guilty. Your killing spree would have had to keep going."

"While it's impressive you're trying to throw the scent off you, it's too late. You are not the only one who was up late last night." Palmer slipped an envelope out of his inside jacket pocket. "I found some things."

Angie sensed this was coming. A few minutes ago she would have welcomed Palmer shifting the blame for everything to McBain but this was a miscalculation. Aaron had just played his hand. Palmer was walking into a trap and dragging her right along behind him. She fidgeted in her chair, thinking to slip out while the accusations were flying.

Aaron clearly had other ideas. He walked over and stood behind her chair with his hands close to her shoulders.

"I had a feeling you'd been busy last night," he said to Palmer but could have been talking to any of them.

Palmer turned to his boss. "McBain has been the threat all along. He sent the warnings to get you to hire him and when he realized you were about to let him go, he devised a plan of revenge."

Lowell drew in a huge breath, then let it out with a loud sigh. Phones rang in the hallway and muffled conversation filtered through the door. No one said anything inside the room, waiting for any response from Lowell, but outside the signs of business life bustled around them.

Finally, he swiveled his chair to face Aaron. "Exactly as you said. He went for you."

Aaron looked apologetic. "Unfortunately, yes."

"What are you two talking about?" Palmer asked.

Lowell shifted his chair back. "Aaron told me about the plans." He stared straight at Angie for an extra second. "Both of you."

Palmer's cool demeanor slipped. He waved his arms and his voice rose. "It's his way of throwing the trail off him. He is telling you what really happened and acting like I'm setting him up. Don't fall for this."

"Because we're so loyal to each other?"

"Yes."

"Speaking of a trail, you left one. You kept changing the potential bad guy in our scenario, which made it easier to track your movements." Aaron moved so that he stood right next to Lowell's chair now. "There were lines of evidence leading to Brandon and to Mark and to your poor conspirator Angie here. You didn't have to time to clean those up before seeing my alive today."

"Of course, you forgot the obvious trail that led to you," Risa said in a quiet voice that somehow managed to ring throughout the room.

"And what was that?" Palmer shot back.

"Max. He's at the police station right now. He's cutting a deal. Once someone explained to him how he could be connected to the murders, he begged for a deal." Aaron put a hand on the back of Lowell's chair and glanced down at him. "He has a tape recording of Palmer's orders."

A roar of fury blared through the room as Palmer

grabbed for his gun. All Angie could think was that they were so close to each other, he and Aaron, that it was hard to imagine anyone missing, especially a trained security agent.

She closed her eyes for a second. When she opened them again, the room was in motion. Aaron shoved Lowell's chair out of the way, spinning him around and blocking any shot with his body. Aaron drew his own weapon. Younger and significantly faster, he got off one shot. Palmer hit the floor before he could pull the trigger.

The small O on his lips faded as Palmer slid to the floor. A red stain spread across his shirt as blood seeped through his fingers. As he lay in a heap and Aaron reached for the phone, the air pumped out of Palmer's chest on staccato breaths.

Lowell shirked out of his jacket and crouched in front of his oldest friend in the world and one of his few in the building. He pressed the wadded-up material to the wound and whispered something that no one but the two of them could hear.

Whatever they said had Palmer shaking his head. He lifted a hand but it fell to the floor as if boneless.

When he spoke, the words were louder. "You ruined everything. Had to go."

Lowell sat back on his heels as his face went pale. "It's my company."

Palmer shook his head, then rode out a spasm of coughing. When he finally stopped, his head rolled to the side and his speech was slurred. "You didn't deserve him."

The words came out harsh between forced pants.

"This has been about Brandon?" Shock filled Lowell's voice.

Palmer nodded and then closed his eyes. "Always. Took him for granted. Destroyed him."

"He's my son."

Angie wanted to scream. All this loss and all this destruction stemmed from Brandon. The kid never did anything in his life and he had people racing around on his behalf.

"You should have stepped down." Palmer grabbed Lowell's sleeve, leaving a bloody handprint on his expensive shirt.

"No, Palmer." Lowell's voice was a mix of resignation and sadness. "You're wrong about this. He doesn't have it."

"Give him the company."

"Never."

But Palmer missed the last answer. He'd passed out.

Angie didn't wait around for the room to turn on her. In the confusion she could sneak out and keep going. She'd packed two bags and emptied a safe-deposit box this morning as a precaution. Good planning always won out.

While the men gathered around Palmer, administering CPR, she grabbed her purse and headed for the door. Watching the scene behind her with each step, she didn't see Risa until she almost ran right over her.

Risa stood in front of the closed office door, ignoring the shouts of people on the other side. "I don't know where you think you're going."

Angie weighed the chances of getting through the woman. Risa weighed less, might be weaker.

She smiled at Angie. "I'm really hoping you try it. I've been dying to unleash some of the new fighting skills I've learned."

In that moment Angie knew she'd lost everything.

Chapter Twenty

The next morning Risa smiled when Aaron slipped his fingers through hers as they walked down the hospital corridor. It felt so right to walk hand in hand.

She wore the jeans and turtleneck black sweater she'd fetched from her apartment when they'd swung by earlier that morning. And he had on the most casual outfit she'd ever seen him in—black jeans and a button-down shirt.

At this point she wondered if he owned normal jeans. But she couldn't deny he looked great in these sexy black ones. She also knew getting him out of them later wouldn't take much effort on her part at all. For a guy who was a dating slow starter, he'd made up for lost time.

After the harrowing morning in Lowell's office yesterday, she'd wanted to spend the entire day rolling around in bed and eating unhealthy food. Aaron had obliged both passions.

It had been tough to watch the life flow out of Palmer and hear his sad confession that reached back to the loss of his son and his frustration at Lowell's failure to appreciate his own son. In fact, it seemed to have stolen most of her energy. How had a father's love turned into all that horror and sadness? Palmer's broken spirit would stay with her for a long time. It shaped the man. In a way it shaped her, too. She wondered if it would have an impact on Lowell or if he was a lost cause and Brandon would just never experience the love he deserved.

If all those depressing events had darkened her soul yesterday, Aaron's lovemaking had restored it last night. On limited sleep and with more than a little worry piled up in her life, she felt alive today. Filled with energy and feeling that bounce that usually came with the onset of warm weather after a harsh snowy winter.

They'd stayed in a hotel while cleaners took care of the mess back in his condo. Aaron had insisted they needed some pampering from room service and a big bathtub, so they skipped her tiny place with the stand-up shower. She was grateful for his maneuvering because she wasn't sure she'd ever be fully comfortable at his place again, ever see the balcony without remembering a man go over. The bloodstains might be erased by professionals, but she saw them whenever she closed her eyes.

But for Aaron she would try to block it out. Ignore all the negative and focus on what the past few days had provided her. She'd never dreamed of another date with Aaron let alone a chance of a lifetime. She would do just about anything for him. Not be his doormat or the woman he held on the side for the rest of his life—she deserved better than that—but if they could build something together, she would.

That's what happened when a woman fell for a great guy. A guy she could trust. Aaron wouldn't run off or take her money. He was solid. Maybe a little slow in the dating department, but solid.

Machines beeped around them as the loudspeaker rang with the newest call for assistance. While she'd enjoyed the hotel, the hospital was a different story. She'd spent more time in this place in the past few days than she had in twenty years.

Most important to her was who wasn't there. Royal was home now, complaining and texting Aaron every few minutes begging for a beer and burger run. He'd actually demanded pizza only to write back and say his wife had forbade it. Aaron had explained that forbidding included couch sleeping in Royal's house, so Royal would be skipping that entrée for some time.

She hadn't met Gail. That would happen during a home visit with Royal later today, but Risa already liked the other woman. Royal and Gail proved the adage that you could measure a person by his friends. Solid, every last one of them.

They walked the hallway to Brandon's private room. Lowell stepped out just as they got there. His tie hung open and his jacket appeared loose over the shoulders, as if he'd lost a significant amount of weight while he waited for Brandon to get better.

Lowell closed the door behind him as he stepped into the hall. "Sonya is visiting. They could use some privacy and a few minutes without me."

Risa didn't really believe people could change overnight. She thought personalities were set; certainly they held a rigidity once a person hit the fifties.

But the man before her no longer had this larger-than-life persona that entered a room a second before he did. He wasn't pontificating and judging. He was trying to act the role of father, which might prove to be the toughest battle of his impressive career.

"How is Brandon doing?" she asked.

The lines across his forehead smoothed out at the mention of his son's name. "Better. He came out of the coma. He's aware of what's going on around him but only has limited memories of that night."

Risa almost envied Brandon that memory loss. Maybe the brain repaired what the body couldn't. By blocking it, he didn't have to relive every minute as she kept doing.

"The doctors are now saying he can go home tomorrow. There will be home therapy and memory work, but we have the resources to get help." Lowell raked a hand through his hair. The strands of gray appeared more pronounced now, and a weariness pulsed all around him.

Aaron shook his hand. "That's all good news. Much better than I think any of us expected so soon."

"We had to tell him about Palmer. Brandon knows he died. He doesn't know the details, but he will eventually. He's a grown man. I can't hide this stuff from him like I did when he was a kid."

A breakthrough. Risa didn't know what else to call it when a man woke up and realized his son was no longer a kid. She hoped that meant good things for the relationship. If nothing else, maybe they could find some sort of tentative peace.

As for Palmer, a heart attack on the way to the hospital had taken his life. Risa guessed he would have survived Aaron's bullet, but he'd never gotten the chance to try. She also assumed Lowell was really talking about telling Brandon about Palmer's part in the bombings and threats.

"About what happened in the office—" Lowell's sentence stopped and he didn't show any signs of finishing it.

She tensed, waiting for him to make a judgment on Aaron's shooting Palmer. Aaron shot because he had to. She knew that as much as she knew anything about her own life. As he'd inched toward Lowell's chair, Risa had panicked thinking the scene would play out a very different way.

He'd been prepared to be a human shield. That's why he stood there. He knew Palmer would make a desperate move.

She'd tried to get Aaron to admit it all, but he'd just shrugged. Hero worship was not his thing, so she practiced it in silence.

Lowell finally looked up at Aaron. "Thank you."

Aaron's eyebrows lifted.

She felt as if she'd been kicked in the gut. Hearing those simple words stunned her. From what she knew about Lowelll, all she'd read and heard, he wasn't a man who appreciated much other than his own steady rise to power. Those who didn't match his drive or talent got left behind.

He didn't leave a lot of room for emotion in business, so sparing some for Aaron meant something. It filled her with pride. She guessed it gave Aaron a sense of accomplishment. How could it not?

Her pride for Aaron and what he stood for, for all the accolades he earned, exploded inside her. He was a good man. And she was a lucky woman.

Aaron opened his mouth, but Lowell held up a hand to stop him. "You didn't have to play it that way. You certainly didn't have to put your body in front of mine. Anything could have happened."

"I don't miss that close."

"But you bleed just like everyone else."

Risa closed her eyes on the horrible thought. When she opened them again Lowell was staring at her. Some of the harsh shadows had left his eyes.

He shook her hand. "And you were pretty impressive, as well."

"It comes with the girlfriend job." She'd spent her entire grown-up life hating that word. It sounded so juvenile, as if she'd been transported back to ninth grade. When she said it about Aaron it made her smile.

Love was a silly, stupid thing.

And that's what it was. She'd known him for such a short time, but she recognized the feeling. The rush of breath when she saw him. The tumble of her stomach right before he kissed her. The thud of her heart when he stripped off his shirt.

She wanted to be with him, talk to him, learn all about him. If she managed not to scare him away, she might have a chance to do all of that.

"And an additional thank-you for keeping quiet about the Angie situation." Lowell's cheeks flushed when he said the words.

"What's going to happen?" Yeah, she should have let it drop, but Risa asked because the curiosity was eating at her.

"She's trying to work a deal. There have been more threats and comments my attorneys assure me amount to blackmail." Lowell stared at his son's door for a second. "When he's up and going again, I'll tell Sonya. She won't be surprised, but at least that way we can take the sting out of Angie's supposed upper hand."

Risa couldn't imagine a marriage based on nothing more than a financial contract. The cold comfort of having someone else in the house but not having love or intimacy sounded like a nightmare to her.

Accepting infidelity was not something she would ever do. Things went wrong, but some aspects of a relationship were sacred and that was one. She glanced at Aaron, saw his strong profile and knew in her heart that was a lecture she'd never have to give him. Besides that, he had a good marriage influence in Royal and she was grateful for that luck.

"We'll let you go," Aaron said. "You can get back to the family and a few days without any danger."

"After all, Christmas is right around the corner." Lowell smiled at her comment but didn't respond.

Aaron slipped his arm around her waist. He shifted her for a quick exit and she didn't fight it.

"There has to be something I can do for you," Lowell said before they'd taken a step.

Aaron pretended to think about it. "Pay your bill."

"Done, and if you're looking for a new job, I have one for waiting you. You would be a fine addition at Craft, especially now that the danger has passed."

Risa struggled to hide her frown. She almost made an unpleasant noise but managed to hold it in. Seeing Lowell now broke her heart. Despite that, the idea of sending Aaron off to work with Lowell each day made her breakfast curdle in her stomach. He was wounded now but his terrible reputation was hard to forget.

"I like being my own boss," Aaron finally said.

"The deal is always open."

"A man couldn't ask for more than that."

Risa thought he could ask for one more thing. Something from her. If he did, she'd give it to him. She was his. Question was whether he realized that yet.

Chapter Twenty-One

By the end of the day, Aaron was dead tired. He tried to remember another point in his life when he'd fired his weapon this much. He'd be filling out forms for months over this job. The insurance company might send someone to shadow him for a month, although he hoped that threat from his agent was a joke.

As it was, the police had all sorts of questions for him. Apparently finding injured men in bathrooms at Elan had not made them happy. The dead guy in the elevator didn't help. Hey, he'd warned them before they fanned out through the building.

Both of the bathroom attackers lived, but one was in critical condition from the loss of blood. The kid on the fifth floor had rubbed his wrists raw but was otherwise okay. As far as Aaron was concerned, the dead guys deserved to be dead.

He opened the hotel room door and ushered Risa inside. With her usual flair, she made a dramatic noise and threw her body across the bed. She plopped down there with her arms and hair spread out over the comforter.

The woman sure did like her comfort. Aaron knew that from just a few days of nonstop togetherness. She never demanded, but somehow she made sure she had

soft pillows and even softer linens. She insisted the bub-
ble bath had been a bonus for him.

Mighty sweet of her to think of him while naked.

She made a delicious picture. So beautiful and full
of life. After seeing so much death, she was a burst of
sunshine.

He marveled at how she'd taken all the threats and
violence in stride. He kept waiting for some blowback.
He'd never known a civilian not to experience after-
effects, even some sort of a posttraumatic reaction.
Some just wanted to talk about the situation until he
thought his head would explode. The need to relive it
was one of his least favorite, so he was grateful she
didn't feel that need.

Whatever he was looking for, whatever symptoms,
never came. She shared all the time, so it was hard to
see how she could keep something that big from him.

Just one more way she surprised him. She was nothing like Pam or any other woman he'd ever known. The
combination of strong, smart and sexy kept knocking
him off balance.

If she ever realized how much power she had over
him, he was a dead man.

Truth was, she had every right to hate him. Some
days when he looked in the mirror he felt a kick of disgust. Taking her to Lowell's office yesterday had been
a mistake. The police had been involved by then and
she would have been safe on her own. He just hated the
idea of being separated from her.

She spread out on the bed until her fingers and toes
touched each end of the mattress. "So, now what?"

"We stick around here, sleep for a month and then
eventually, when we think all the gunman have cleared
out, we try having dinner again."

She lifted her head and glared at him. "That gunman thing isn't funny."

Worse for her, he was only half kidding on that one. Thanks to the constant attacks on her, he now expected someone to jump out around every corner.

It wasn't a bad worry to have. It kept him fresh and ready to go. He could be on the defensive and easily switch to the offensive if his battle gear was always ready to go.

"I promise no gunmen for a while."

She flopped back down. "That's good news, but I wasn't talking about anything so specific."

He sat down on the bed and ran his fingers over her thigh. "What were we talking about?"

"Do you think we're going to pick up where we left off?"

He'd hoped they had fast-forwarded well past that point. He'd go back to chaste kisses and wooing if she needed that, but he much preferred the heated love-making.

He went for a joke because he thought that's what she wanted. "Don't tell me I'm still in trouble for not calling you sooner."

"I was thinking we skip ahead and I don't just mean in the physical sense."

He let his fingers trail off her leg and onto the bed. "Okay."

She scooted until she balanced on her elbows behind her. "Which I take it is some sort of male code for 'time to run' because that's what it sounds like."

"You're jumping to conclusions."

"Am I?"

"I don't understand what's happening here." They'd morphed from light banter to a serious conversation.

He had no idea where this was going or how to put on the brakes before it veered into danger territory. It had already crossed that line.

"Apparently."

This had to be a male-female thing. That would explain his complete loss for how to navigate through this patch. He was still trying to figure out how they'd even wandered into this patch.

"Can you clue me in as to what you want? What are we talking about? I am a black-and-white guy. If I know what you want, I'll try to give it to you." Within reason, and that was the caveat that frequently killed the deal.

Her dark-eyed gaze searched his face. The frown and scrunch of her forehead suggested this was very serious to her.

He was desperate not to get this wrong.

She sat the whole way up, crossing her legs in that pretzel position women loved and men couldn't conquer without a shoehorn and a lot of screaming. "If I asked you to come to my office holiday party with me, what would you say?"

He could not think of anything in the world he wanted to do less than venture to another party. If he had his way they'd postpone Christmas until he got caught up and Elan was a distant memory.

"You're still having one after all of this? If I saw a Christmas tree right about now, I might shoot it. Same goes for angels, trumpets and bells."

"Humor me."

He wasn't sure what answer she wanted. He'd hoped honesty would score some points. Amazing how often it didn't in a world that professed to hold it up as a prize. "Well, it's not really my thing."

She picked at the comforter. As the quiet stretched, the plucking grew rough enough to rip the fabric.

"Not your thing?" She mimicked his tone as she said it.

Uh-oh.

"I'm not one for committed couple's activities. Dinner parties, brunch, going home to meet the family. It's not my style."

The words weren't even out of his mouth before he realized how asinine they sounded. Calling them back wouldn't work. He debated if adding more might clean it up.

But she was already pulling away. She shifted and let her feet fall to the floor on the opposite side of the bed. "I don't have any family."

The words sliced through him. He hadn't even thought about it enough to be careful, which was obvious by the way he threw it out there. "Sorry. That was insensitive."

When she stared at him with flat eyes, he tried again. "Look, I—"

She stood up. Her head fell to the side, and her arms slipped across her stomach. It was the least receptive stance he'd ever seen from her. She closed everything off from him. Even her bright eyes and sunny face seemed to have dimmed in his presence.

"You want to know what I think?"

Worst. Question. Ever.

"Not when you say it like that."

"I think you're afraid."

The fight behind the words shattered what was left of their calm existence. She wanted a reaction. That much was clear. Well, she got one. She could have a fight if she wanted one of those, too.

He slowly got to his feet. "Excuse me?"

"A woman hurt you and instead of writing her off as the wrong person for you, you've decided to remove yourself from the dating pool."

She tapped her foot. He could hear it across the room on carpet. That had to be a bad thing.

Little did she know or want to understand, but Pam was the last person on his mind right now. He was having more than enough trouble with the woman in front of him. He didn't need to add another to his list of responsibilities.

"That is in the past," he said. "That relationship isn't about us."

"The breakup is who you are."

That would make him a victim, and he refused to be that. He didn't wallow. He wasn't like his client, who refused to move on. "That is absolutely not true."

"How else can I see this?"

He didn't even understand what they were arguing about. To him, the topic kept jumping around, half the time landing on unrelated issues. "That we're dating."

"Meaning?"

He felt ridiculous spelling out the obvious. "We've gone out. Hell, we've stayed in. So I don't think your theory about me hating dating applies here."

"But you intended to keep it casual." She threw her hands up in the air. "You never even called me back for another date. Without a shoot-out at Elan, I'd still be waiting to hear from you."

He was going to pay for this forever. "We're back to this? I said I was sorry. I can say it again."

"Don't bother." She waved him off and went to the chair.

He couldn't see what she was doing until he heard

the zipper of a suitcase. He scanned the room for her clothes and missed the usual stray sock or shoe that usually sat in the middle of the room.

She was leaving and he had no idea why she was even angry.

"Why are we fighting?"

She picked up the suitcase, then threw it back down again. When she faced him, her eyes flashed with fire. Stress showed in every line of her body. Clenched fists and a flat mouth.

Nothing about her was open or receptive to anything other than a yelling battle. Shame he had no intention of playing along.

"I bet if all of this hadn't happened, you would have found a different place to have coffee. One where you calculated you had the lowest risk of running into me. After all, the D.C. area is pretty big. If you hid and ran, I wouldn't have been able to find you. I'd have been looking for a tax attorney who didn't exist."

The comment knocked him speechless.

But not for long.

Suddenly everything was his fault. Unfortunately for her, he'd picked that same moment to run out of patience. "Would you have looked?"

"Probably not back then. I didn't really know you."

Exactly. "Well, then, what's the point?"

"That was before everything happened. Before we were on the run together." She grabbed the bag with both hands and hugged it to her chest.

The defiant look had him backing off. So did the idea of her walking out. His mind shut down at the idea.

"Adrenaline is powerful," he said.

"So is love."

Silence fell over the room. He stood there all open-mouthed and stupid. She huffed and puffed.

They made a curious pair.

He tried to think of something to say. For a way for his mind to process the words so they didn't just hang out there. "Risa…"

"Yeah, if you weren't terrified before, I bet you are now."

He rubbed his chest. The heaviness refused to ease. "Maybe you could stop taking shots at my level of courage."

"Oh, you're great with weapons and anything that involves taking out bad guys. It's the intimacy part that makes you run screaming for cover." Her hands dropped to her sides. In one of them she held a suitcase.

It was her ticket out, back home and away from him. He knew that as sure as if she'd said it out loud.

He tried his last bit of logic. This was about timing, not feelings. He had to convince her of that. "We've only known each other for a short time."

"I don't think the number of hours means anything." She discounted the idea as quickly as he raised it. "You think I planned to fall for you? I had a man lie to me and turn my life upside down. I am still rebuilding from the fallout."

She had just turned around and proved his point. They needed time, maybe a bit of space. He wanted to be with her, but he didn't want the walls to close in. He didn't want her to see something better away from him.

The ache in his chest ripped as he moved to her. It was as if he'd been sliced open and the gaping wound grew with every step. "See, it's too early—"

"When a second man came into my life, telling lies and dodging his feelings, you'd think I'd have been smart enough to run, but the exact opposite happened. I want to stay and fight for you. For us."

That fast, the pain turned to a red-hot anger. "Do not compare me to Paul."

"Because you didn't take my money?" She threw back her head and laughed. "Oh, Aaron, what you did is so much worse. You grabbed my heart and now you're too afraid to hold on to it."

The words punched into him. "You're moving fast."

"I'm moving forward. I'm ready. I'd hoped you were, too, but I guess not."

"How did this situation become my fault?"

"It isn't. You're right."

The tone of her voice changed. He wanted to think he was winning her over, but he feared she was giving up.

She hadn't moved. Hadn't come to him or reached out with any part of her. She was closed to him, something that had never happened before, not even when she learned he wasn't who he claimed to be.

He tried to swallow, but his mouth was too dry. "We should calm down and think about this logically."

"You never made me a promise. I'm the one who rushed to fill in the blanks." She rubbed her cheeks and under her eyes.

Tears. The reality of her pain, that he inflicted it, sliced through him with the horrifying rip of a blade. "Please don't cry."

"I'm saying goodbye."

The words shredded him as much as the tears. "Why does this have to be a forever-or-never issue?"

She rounded the bed with the suitcase in her hand. "If I thought, for even one second, that there was hope you'd put the past behind you and trust me with your future, I would ask you where you wanted to go for dinner."

"Then we're fine." He reached out. When she didn't shrink away from him, he let his hands settle on her arms. Let her warmth seep into him.

"You're saying words you don't mean."

The hollowness in his stomach spilled over to the rest of him. "I hate when women do that, when they think they know what you feel and assume."

She gave him a watery smile. "I'm just one of the 'women' now?"

"That's not what I meant."

"I can promise you I'll never try to change your love for your job. Guarantee that I won't make you choose. That I will always love you. But none of that matters if you don't believe." She kept the stranglehold on the suitcase and never touched him.

"I do trust you." He said the words and meant them. He trusted her more than he'd ever trusted another woman.

She lifted her hand then. Her fingers traced his cheek to his jawline. "You are this smart and dedicated, strong and sexy man. But you have this wall around you, and while I am willing to climb over it, I need help."

The words didn't make any sense to him. He was offering her all he had. "You are making this so much more complicated than it needs to be."

"No, I'm making everything very easy. You can go back to your life exactly as you like it—alone and safe."

"That's not fair."

She leaned in and kissed his cheek. The touch was gone almost before it started. "Merry Christmas, Aaron. I hope you get everything you want."

His hand dropped from her arm as she turned away. "Risa, don't do this."

"Goodbye."

Chapter Twenty-Two

After a week without Risa, Aaron was slowly going mad. Though she'd barely been in his condo, he smelled her when he walked in the door each night. He saw her, or visions of her, on the street. He even listened to her last voice mail over and over to remember her voice.

He had it bad.

Royal sat at his desk and stared Aaron down. "Man, if you don't smarten up soon I'm quitting."

He'd been back in the office for four days. He didn't let a little thing like surgery and almost being blown into a million pieces slow down his work schedule. Royal wanted his life back and insisted that happen immediately.

Then he came in, ribs wrapped and limping, and demanded to know where Risa was. He'd been asking questions about her ever since. The two times Aaron complained, Royal blamed the interest on Gail.

"I may leave anyway," Royal grumbled. "It would serve you right."

"What's that supposed to mean?" Aaron asked, but he knew. Royal had been dropping hints at his displeasure over his boss's love life every ten to twelve seconds.

"Take it from a long-married man—"

This counted as Aaron's least favorite lecture. "You got married before you were legally able to drink."

Royal pointed at Aaron. "And I'm still with the same woman, and will be forever, so the start date of the relationship isn't relevant. Neither is how long you've known each other before you know she's the one."

Now he sounded like Risa. "Subtle."

"Go to her. Get on your knees, beg for forgiveness and stop kicking around here." Royal moved around too much, then grabbed his side on a wince.

"It's not that easy."

Two days ago when Royal had said the same thing, Aaron told him where he could go. Hearing the advice a second time now, Aaron could think if nothing but that it might not be enough to get Risa back.

He'd gone from being firm in his position to wavering. He was ready to chuck whatever complaints he could think of if it meant she'd give him ten minutes to plead his case.

"Of course it is. Christmas is next week. Do you really want to go through another holiday season alone?"

How had the holiday snuck up like that? The last thing he cared about was gifts and trees.

"I ticked her off." The words popped out. Normally he wouldn't share on this level with Royal, but all the arguments and frustrations were locked inside him and Aaron needed them out.

Royal leaned his chair back and stared at the ceiling. "You're ticking me off."

"We have work to do."

His chair legs hit the floor again. "Let me ask you something."

Aaron pretended to file. He'd done that a lot lately. "Can I say no?"

"Is there anything on your desk or anywhere in this office that matters to you more than Risa?"

Aaron slammed the desk drawer shut. "No."

"Then go fix your mess."

When he put it like that, it did sound easy. Pretty satisfying, too. Sleeping alone sure wasn't.

And it wasn't just the sex. He'd turned over a thousand times during the past week, thinking to tell her something and she wasn't there. How a woman who spent so little time in his life could come to mean so much confused him.

He struggled to bring common sense back into the equation. The last time he'd led only with his heart, he ended up with a woman who dumped him. "I need to think this through. If I rush in I run the risk of disappointing us both."

Royal nodded. "Absolutely. That makes sense."

Aaron wasn't expecting the agreement. "Right."

"Good."

Was it? "It's the smart way to proceed."

Royal held up a finger. "One thing, though."

"What?"

"She works with pretty much all men, right?"

Aaron didn't like where this was headed. The chest ache he got every time he thought about her thundered back. "Where are you going with this?"

"Nowhere."

"Okay, then." Aaron stared at the papers in front of them. He had no idea what they said. His vision clouded until all the black ink ran together.

The silence lasted all of three seconds.

"It just seems to me the combination of men, mistletoe and the holidays could be tempting, especially if she's looking for a way to forget you or even get back at you." Royal reached for the soda on the far side of his desk and hissed when he couldn't grab it. "You might want to be careful about how long you wait."

That did it. Not having her ripped him up inside until he bled. Thinking of her with someone else shredded him further. It would also guarantee jail time because he'd kill anyone who touched her. It wasn't rational and might not even be right, but he knew how he felt and that was it.

Aaron stood up, stopped by Royal's desk to slide the can closer. "I'm leaving for the day."

The guy sighed with delight. "Thought so."

"I'm taking some vacation time." Aaron got the whole way to the door before he turned back. "And, Royal?"

"Huh?"

"Thanks." Maybe Risa was right about something else. Royal would make the perfect business partner.

THAT FRIDAY, RISA HOVERED by the eggnog bowl and watched her coworkers laugh as they fought over the remaining Christmas cookies. They joked. A few sang.

Who knew engineers loved sugar cookies in the shape of stockings?

Finding out she had almost died all in the name of locating the ultimate holiday party location made her the office star. When they insisted on changing the venue to the office, the relief crashing through her nearly knocked her off her feet. The idea of going back to Elan made her stomach heave.

Not that Elan was an option. They'd managed to blow that place apart. Literally.

The soft opening had turned into an early closing. A full renovation of the brand-new facility was now necessary. There was talk of waiting until spring to try again. Some reporters suggested a name change.

The general view was the place was cursed. It didn't help that one article talked about dead bodies on every floor. That was an exaggeration, of course, but every time people told the story it seemed to get worse. Having lived it, she wouldn't have said that was possible.

Personally, she wanted to petition to shut the place down permanently. Revisiting the terror and uncertainty was her nightmare, and she wouldn't let it happen. Being in the place where her feelings for Aaron had exploded into love sounded just as awful.

She wanted to forget. She'd played every mind trick she could think of to push the image of his face out of her head, to erase the memories and rewind to the moment right before she met him. Nothing worked.

She'd picked up the phone to call him so many times since their last rough encounter. Leaving that hotel had been the hardest decision of her life. Some part of her, that romantic part deep inside, had hoped he'd follow. The idea seemed ludicrous now, but it hadn't been then.

Realizing he wasn't the type for a grand gesture, she was sometimes tempted to give in and let their relationship meander along the way Aaron wanted. Maybe he really did need time and space. Or maybe she was just sad and pathetic.

Seeing happy couples and all the holiday decorations didn't help. The holiday season was a killer for a person in love and alone.

He wanted the strings loose. She weighed the pros and cons of letting that happen, but in every scenario he treaded water and she got her heart broken.

A reluctant smile curled her lips when two guys wrestled for the microphone on a carol singing dare.

The cameras came out and the bragging grew to Big Band levels. Her coworkers made it all bearable.

A weight pressed against her back. She was about to push away and send a have-you-lost-your-mind? glare when the husky voice broke through the celebration and touched like a kiss against the back of her neck.

"Are they always this loud?"

"Aaron?" She spun around to face him.

He continued to watch the festivities. He wore dress pants and a sweater as he rocked back on his heels. His handsome face was even more breathtaking than she remembered, even with the shadowed valleys under his eyes.

His hands stayed in his back pants pockets. "You may need a bouncer."

The party blended into the background. The sounds and lights faded away until all she saw was him. "What are you doing here?"

He looked at her then. Those blue-green eyes held both sadness and a flicker of an emotion she couldn't identify. "You asked me to be your date."

Her heart leaped, but she ignored it. "That was before."

His eyebrow lifted along with his mouth. "Before I was a jackass?"

"I… Well, yeah."

"Dance with me." He held out a hand and nodded toward the now-empty dance floor. The engineers liked to sing but, apparently, not to dance.

The sharp change in direction caught her by surprise. She never expected to see him here, in this environment. She absolutely didn't expect for him to offer his services as his date.

But touching him… She'd been dreaming about that

for days. Her wavering control would take a hike if she let him get close.

For her self-protection, she gave him the answer she didn't want to say. "I don't think that's a good idea."

"But I want to touch you."

Yep, the man knew just what to say. It wasn't just her heart jumping around inside her. She'd bet every internal organ was up and spinning around. "I have no idea what to say to that."

"How about yes?" He slipped his fingers through hers in the intimate hold she loved so much.

Before common sense could kick in and ruin everything she gave in. "Okay."

She fell into his arms as if she were born to be there. Her hand went to his biceps, and his palm slid to her lower back. The press of his fingers against the thin material of her dress touched off a flash of memories, all of them welcome and more than a few X-rated. If her mind wandered down that lane too far, she'd be blushing.

"This is a nice place." He bent his head close to hers.

Her breath caught in her throat. She tried to push it out, but it just hung there as if waiting for him to take it from her. "I love it here."

She loved him. Every single thing about him. The way he smelled. The way he held her. The promise of his kiss and the staking of a claim in his hold.

He continued to dance them in a circle. Their feet moved in time with the music. Like with everything else he did, he was good at dancing. Could keep a beat and knew how to lead.

"The company suits you. The mood fits your personality."

Her mind spun off and his conversation kept to the

mundane. Much more of this and she'd go insane. She stepped back, putting a bit of air between them.

Though meeting his gaze without melting proved difficult, she looked up at him. "Aaron, honestly, I have no idea what we're doing here."

He stopped moving but didn't let go of her. "I'm groveling."

She must have misheard. "What?"

"See, I'm not afraid of much in this world. I carry the gun, issue orders and generally stay in control. Dad taught me that. The navy reinforced it. Operating that way more or less guarantees my life runs like I want it to."

She had no clue what any of that had to do with him being there or the dancing. He put pieces together in a way that didn't always make sense to her. "Okay. That's good, I guess."

"It all worked, went along fine or what I grew to believe was fine, until you came along. You mess everything up."

The last flicker of hope blew out.

She dropped her hands and stepped back. She didn't need air between them. She needed a building, possibly a state. "Thanks for stopping by, Aaron, but—"

He didn't move. "You scare the crap out of me because I can't control my feelings for you."

The sentence kept her from storming off the dance floor. "Is that bad?"

Some of the tension left his face and he smiled. "When I look at you, all my plans blow apart and my brain misfires. I want you in bed and then with me at the table the next morning. I look at every aspect of my life and see room for you."

She finally recognized that compelling look in his

eyes—hope. She felt it. It burst to life in the room, filling it to the rafters.

Daring to believe was a huge risk, and she wasn't ready to go there yet. "You do?"

"Then you walked out and I learned what a huge sucking void you leave when you exit a room. Every part of me ached." He closed his eyes and when he opened them again, a storm raged in them. Whatever he battled inside him showed on the outside. "It's about missing you. About rolling over in bed and wanting to hold you and you're not there."

She closed the gap between them. Her arms went around his neck and his lips brushed against her hair. "Aaron."

It was as if he'd been waiting for her touch. Now that he had it, he crushed her against him. She glanced up to see the whole room watching. The engineers lined up, most of them smiling. She doubted they even knew she had a boyfriend. Not a surprise since ten minutes ago she hadn't thought she did, either.

Aaron shrugged as his face lit up with a look she could only describe as happiness. "They can listen in. I don't care who knows."

"Since when?"

He had always struck her as such a private man. The idea of him making a public declaration, of him welcoming the other people into their relationship was huge. It was him telling the world they were together. This wasn't a casual thing. This was an actual thing.

He cupped her face in his hands. "Since I realized loving you means not being in control all the time."

The bottom fell out of her stomach. Her mouth moved, but no words came out.

It took his smile and the sweet light smiling in his eyes to give her the confidence. "Love?"

He nodded. "Did you really not know?"

Waves of happiness crashed over her. She felt sunny and alive and happier than she'd ever been.

Her hands roamed over his back as her gaze caressed his face. "I hoped. I certainly didn't think you knew."

"Admittedly I was slow on this one. I'd see you and feel this tug. We'd go out and the tug turned to a yanking pull. I didn't know what it was, so I ran from it."

"And now?"

He kissed her then. A hot mouth and a soft touch filled with promise. Without words he told her how much he cared. It was in his hold and the way his lips slanted over hers.

When he lifted his head she saw the love. She had no idea how anyone could miss it.

"I'm so tired of running, of being alone and without you, of pretending I don't feel something. I want to celebrate Christmas with you, take you home to meet my dad, who is going to love you, and then start the New Year with you in my arms."

Any one of those things would have been perfect. He was pushing past his personal boundaries and taking her to the place she wanted to go. To where they needed to be.

"You are saying all the right things."

"Better than that, I'm feeling them." He pressed his forehead against hers. "Consider it a vow. A promise of forever."

She could hear the engineers talking. Some were asking about the guy in her arms. Others were demanding an introduction. They'd get to all of it, but she wanted him to herself first.

"That's the best Christmas gift. I'd give up everything else for your love." She kissed him again because not doing so was killing her.

"That's the thing, Risa." He set her slightly away from him, but not far away that anything could come between them. "You don't have to give up anything. I'm ready to hand you everything you need and want. All I ask is that you keep on loving this hardheaded man through his stupidity and cluelessness."

She jumped into his arms, knowing he'd catch her tight against his body. "Give me one more dance and I'll let you take me home and we can try some of that loving there."

"The plan is to give your coworkers an extra thrill by steering this dance under the mistletoe for a bit of a show."

She didn't say no. She kissed him right there instead. When they finally lifted their heads she thought she heard some clapping.

"Merry Christmas, baby." He whispered the words against her lips.

"You're early."

"No, I'd say I finally got the timing just right."

* * * * *

COMING NEXT MONTH from Harlequin® Intrigue®
AVAILABLE NOVEMBER 27, 2012

#1389 CHRISTMAS RESCUE AT MUSTANG RIDGE
Delores Fossen

To find a bone marrow donor for his child, Sheriff Jake McCall must hack into witness protection files to locate Maggie Gallagher, the last woman he ever expected to see again.

#1390 COWBOY COP
Bucking Bronc Lodge
Rita Herron

A little boy in jeopardy, a father who will do anything to protect him and a tenderhearted woman who has nothing to lose but her heart when she tries to help them.

#1391 THREE COWBOYS
3-in-1
Julie Miller, Dana Marton and Paula Graves

With their family in danger, the McCabe brothers are forced to return home to Texas for Christmas. Once there, they meet their match in a vicious criminal...and three irresistible women.

#1392 MONTANA REFUGE
The Legacy
Alice Sharpe

With a murderer on her trail, Julie Hunt can think of only one place to seek refuge—with the cowboy she walked away from a year before.

#1393 THE AWAKENING
Mystere Parish
Jana DeLeon

Although detective Tanner LeDoux tempted her in ways she'd sworn to avoid, Josie Bettencourt wasn't about to let a mysterious legend prevent her from saving her family home.

#1394 SECRETS OF THE LYNX
Copper Canyon
Aimée Thurlo

Kendra Armstrong had given up on love and almost given up on her biggest case to date...until Paul Greyhorse joined her in a search for a dangerous sniper.

You can find more information on upcoming Harlequin® titles, free excerpts and more at www.Harlequin.com.

HICNM1112

REQUEST YOUR FREE BOOKS!
2 FREE NOVELS PLUS 2 FREE GIFTS!

Harlequin®

INTRIGUE®

BREATHTAKING ROMANTIC SUSPENSE

YES! Please send me 2 FREE Harlequin Intrigue® novels and my 2 FREE gifts (gifts are worth about $10). After receiving them, if I don't wish to receive any more books, I can return the shipping statement marked "cancel." If I don't cancel, I will receive 6 brand-new novels every month and be billed just $4.49 per book in the U.S. or $5.24 per book in Canada. That's a saving of at least 14% off the cover price! It's quite a bargain! Shipping and handling is just 50¢ per book in the U.S. and 75¢ per book in Canada.* I understand that accepting the 2 free books and gifts places me under no obligation to buy anything. I can always return a shipment and cancel at any time. Even if I never buy another book, the two free books and gifts are mine to keep forever.

182/382 HDN FEQ2

Name	(PLEASE PRINT)	
Address		Apt. #
City	State/Prov.	Zip/Postal Code

Signature (if under 18, a parent or guardian must sign)

Mail to the **Reader Service:**
IN U.S.A.: P.O. Box 1867, Buffalo, NY 14240-1867
IN CANADA: P.O. Box 609, Fort Erie, Ontario L2A 5X3

Not valid for current subscribers to Harlequin Intrigue books.

**Are you a subscriber to Harlequin Intrigue books
and want to receive the larger-print edition?
Call 1-800-873-8635 or visit www.ReaderService.com.**

* Terms and prices subject to change without notice. Prices do not include applicable taxes. Sales tax applicable in N.Y. Canadian residents will be charged applicable taxes. Offer not valid in Quebec. This offer is limited to one order per household. All orders subject to credit approval. Credit or debit balances in a customer's account(s) may be offset by any other outstanding balance owed by or to the customer. Please allow 4 to 6 weeks for delivery. Offer available while quantities last.

Your Privacy—The Reader Service is committed to protecting your privacy. Our Privacy Policy is available online at www.ReaderService.com or upon request from the Reader Service.

We make a portion of our mailing list available to reputable third parties that offer products we believe may interest you. If you prefer that we not exchange your name with third parties, or if you wish to clarify or modify your communication preferences, please visit us at www.ReaderService.com/consumerchoice or write to us at Reader Service Preference Service, P.O. Box 9062, Buffalo, NY 14269. Include your complete name and address.

HI11B

HARLEQUIN

ROMANTIC
SUSPENSE

Get your heart racing this holiday season with double the pulse-pounding action.

Christmas Confidential

Featuring

Holiday Protector by **Marilyn Pappano**

Miri Duncan doesn't care that it's almost Christmas. She's got bigger worries on her mind. But surviving the trip to Georgia from Texas is going to be her biggest challenge. Days in a car with the man who broke her heart and helped send her to prison—private investigator Dean Montgomery.

A Chance Reunion by **Linda Conrad**

When the husband Elana Novak left behind five years ago shows up in her new California home she knows danger is coming her way. To protect the man she is quickly falling for Elana must convince private investigator Gage Chance that she is a different person. But Gage isn't about to let her walk away…even with the bad guys right on their heels.

Available December 2012 wherever books are sold!

Special excerpt from Harlequin Nocturne

*In a time of war between humans and vampires,
the only hope of peace lies in the love between
mortal enemies Captain Fiona Donnelly
and the deadly vampire scout Kain....*

*Read on for a sneak peek at "Halfway to Dawn"
by* New York Times *bestselling author Susan Krinard.*

* * *

Fiona opened her eyes.

The first thing she saw was the watery sunlight filtering through the waxy leaves of the live oak above her. The first thing she remembered was the bloodsuckers roaring and staggering about, drunk on her blood.

And then the sounds of violence, followed by quiet and the murmuring of voices. A strong but gentle touch. Faces…

Nightsiders.

No more than a few feet away, she saw two men huddled under the intertwined branches of a small thicket.

Vassals. That was what they had called themselves. But they were still Nightsiders. They wouldn't try to move until sunset. She could escape. All she had to do was find enough strength to get up.

"Fiona."

The voice. The calm baritone that had urged her to be still, to let him…

Her hand flew to her neck. It was tender, but she could feel nothing but a slight scar where the ugly wounds had been.

"Fiona," the voice said again. Firm but easy, like that of a man used to command and too certain of his own masculinity to fear compassion. The man emerged from the thicket.

He was unquestionably handsome, though there were deep shadows under his eyes and cheekbones. He wore only a shirt against the cold, a shirt that revealed the breadth of his shoulders and the fitness of his body. A soldier's body.

"It's all right," the man said, raising his hand. "The ones who attacked you are dead, but you shouldn't move yet. Your body needs more time."

"Kain," she said. "Your name is Kain."

He nodded. "How much do you remember?"

Too much, now that she was fully conscious. Pain, humiliation, growing weakness as the blood had been drained from her veins.

"Why did you save me? You said you were deserters."

"We want freedom," Kain said, his face hardening. "Just as you do."

Freedom from the Bloodlord or Bloodmaster who virtually owned them. But vassals still formed the majority of the troops who fought for these evil masters.

No matter what these men had done for her, they were still her enemies.

* * *

*Discover the intense conclusion to
"Halfway to Dawn"
by Susan Krinard, featured in
HOLIDAY WITH A VAMPIRE 4,
available November 13, 2012,
from Harlequin® Nocturne™.*